Joseph Hatton, John Lawrence Toole

Reminiscences of John Lawrence Toole

Vol. 2

Joseph Hatton, John Lawrence Toole

Reminiscences of John Lawrence Toole
Vol. 2

ISBN/EAN: 9783337425401

Printed in Europe, USA, Canada, Australia, Japan

Cover: Foto ©Raphael Reischuk / pixelio.de

More available books at **www.hansebooks.com**

REMINISCENCES

OF

J. L. TOOLE

RELATED BY HIMSELF, AND CHRONICLED BY

JOSEPH HATTON,

Author of " Clytie " " Cruel London," " The Gay World," " Christopher Kenrick," " Journalistic London," &c.

ILLUSTRATED BY ALFRED BRYAN AND W. H. MARGETSON.

IN TWO VOLUMES.

VOL. II.

LONDON:

HURST AND BLACKETT, LIMITED,

GREAT MARLBOROUGH STREET.

1889.

CONTENTS OF VOL. II.

I.

NOTABLE BANQUETS.

II.

IN AMERICA.

III.

OUR TRIP TO THE NORTH.

IV.

CHATS BY THE WAY, AND JESTS.

V.

COMBINING BUSINESS WITH PLEASURE.

LIST OF ILLUSTRATIONS TO VOL. II.

REMINISCENCES

OF

J. L. TOOLE, THE COMEDIAN.

I.

NOTABLE BANQUETS.

Mr. Toole's American Tour—"Why Lord Rosebery?"—
Byron and Charles Mathews—A memorable night—A
message from the Prince of Wales—"Success and Long
Life to Mr. Toole"—Lord Rosebery's speech—Mr.
Toole's reply—What Charles Mathews said—Farewell
Dinner at Birmingham—George Dawson on the Stage—
Mr. Toole on George Dawson—The Church and the
Stage.

I.

"THE dinner that was given to me on the eve of
my departure for America, is particularly interesting just now, when Lord Rosebery has won a
prominent position in the councils of his country,
and is a leader among the great parties in the
State ; for he was the chairman, and made on
that occasion, perhaps, his first notable speech at a
public banquet. When he was invited to preside,

and kindly consented to do so, some people asked, 'Why Lord Rosebery?' But some people did

MR. HENRY J. BYRON.

not know what stuff there was in the young noble-man, and many of the best-informed guests on the occasion were agreeably surprised and delighted with him. He had evidently himself heard a hint of the suggestion, 'Why Lord Rosebery ?' because, in the course of his most eloquent and generous address, he gave the company his own views upon the subject. 'I have been probably selected to fill the chair,' he said, 'because I have paid, possibly, more money to see Mr. Toole act than any one of those present.'

"An incident in the evening which amused me very much was the pointed way in which Charles Mathews fired off at poor Byron some of his humorous criticisms about authors. It happened that Byron had just risen from his seat at the moment when Mathews jocularly spoke of the unimportance of the author of a play. 'People don't go to a theatre because So-and-so has written the piece. An author is all very well to sit about and to talk with, but he isn't of any particular importance ; and in Mr. Toole's case it isn't the piece at all—it's the actor.' Mathews nodded at Byron. Byron smiled, and joined in the applause of the speech as it went on.'

---

[1] "By the death of Mr. Henry J. Byron, which took place last Friday evening at his residence, in Clapham, the literature of the contemporary British stage is suddenly, if not altogether unexpectedly, bereft of one of its most prolific, versatile, and diverting contributors. As a dramatic author Mr. Byron, for several years in succession, occupied an exceptional, and in

" It will always be to me a most memorable
night.   I never think of it but with pride and

some respects unprecedented, position with relation to the
metropolitan and provincial stage, his works being in such
general request among managers, and standing so high in
public favour, that comedies, farces, and burlesques from his
fertile and facile pen were being performed at one and the
same time in several leading London theatres and in well-nigh
every country town of considerable importance.   Whilst producing play after play with a rapidity that appeared little less
than marvellous, he was contributing copiously to the lighter
periodical literature of the day, and not infrequently imper-
sonating on the boards one or another of the characters that
were the offspring of his lively imagination.   His humour was
quaint, dry, and somewhat caustic, holding, as a rule, the
happy mean between mere catching obviousness and that
supersubtlety which compels the hearer of a joke to think
seriously before he can permit himself to laugh heartily.   As a
punster, Mr. Byron had few equals, if any, throughout the
period of his greatest productiveness, when his entertaining
burlesques of popular operas and dramas kept crowded
audiences nightly in roars of laughter at the Strand, Prince of
Wales's, Adelphi, and Olympic theatres.   His word-plays,
always ingenious, were now and anon so far-fetched as to convey the impression that they had been thought and wrought
out with extraordinary pains ; but those who knew him best,
and enjoyed the most frequent opportunities of appreciating
his rare conversational gifts, can bear witness that jests of no
ordinary intricacy fell from his lips with a spontaneity every
whit as manifest as that which characterized his quiet, satur-
nine utterance of simpler and more self-suggested funniments.
With respect to his dramatic works of all categories, it is
especially noteworthy—greatly to the honour of the deceased
—that their morality was irreproachable.   Henry Byron was
as pure a writer as the late Charles Dickens himself.   His
plots were never founded upon incidents arising from or lead-

pleasure, except when I think of it with regret for some of the dear fellows who were present and whom we shall see no more.

"A few days afterwards I received a similar compliment—on a smaller scale, of course, but none the less very welcome for the kindly spirit of it—at Birmingham, my dear friend, George Dawson—now, alas! only a memory, but a very sweet and tender one—occupying the chair."

II.

THE London banquet above referred to took place on the 24th of June, 1874, at Willis's Rooms, under the best and brightest auspices. "The original idea," says the *Era*, "of a few friends inviting Mr. J. L. Toole to a dinner, that he might receive formal expression of the good wishes which would accompany him on his professional tour through America, was so warmly and enthusiastically encouraged, wherever it was mentioned,

ing up to violations of the marriage vow; his dialogue was refreshingly free from those unsavoury allusions conventionally designated as *double entendres*, and from the faintest suggestion of indelicacy. He often made his *dramatis personæ* indulge in severe interchanges of chaff that was nothing if not personal; but coarse vulgarity and indecorous innuendo were inflexibly tabooed from every speech spoken by the children of his fancy or indited by his pen for the amusement of the reading public. —*Daily Telegraph*, April 14th, 1884.

that it became necessary to enlarge the modest proposition at first privately made to a plan of much more extensive proportions." The tickets were a guinea and a half each, and were so rapidly taken up that many of the later applicants found it impossible to obtain seats.

The executive committee, whose arrangements were much commended during the evening, were Messrs. Charles Dickens, jun., chairman; Morley D. Longden, secretary; Peter Berlyn, Charles Coote, John Drew, John Hollingshead, Albert Levy, Charles Shaw, H. J. Montagu, Captain Styan, C. F. Pinches, William Tinsley, Thomas J. Thompson, and J. C. Pawle.

"The choice of the Earl of Rosebery," remarks the *Era*, "for president, was the happiest that could be made; and the force and fluency of his speeches, associated with a most winning mode of delivery, called forth the warmest expressions of admiration. Nothing, indeed, was wanting to make the event memorable in the history of the Stage as a splendid acknowledgment of the dignity of the dramatic art."

In proposing the toast of "The Prince and Princess of Wales," the Chairman said :—"Their Royal Highnesses, as is well known, take a warm interest in everything that is English; and I venture to say that there is nothing so English as the drama. (Hear, hear.) But on the present occasion I have a special message to convey from the Prince of Wales, saying how heartily he hopes that our guest may have a prosperous journey to America—(applause)—that no one is more in-

LORD ROSEBERY.

terested than himself in Mr. Toole's success in that new field ; and that he wishes for himself a prosperous and speedy return of our guest back to his native country."

Lord Rosebery, in proposing the toast of the evening, " Success and Long Life to Mr. Toole," said :—" Gentlemen, if ever there was an occasion for a bumper toast, it is the one I am about to propose to you. I have often observed at dinners like the present that, when the viands are good, the company good, and the speeches short, much enjoyment is derived by everybody except two persons, and they are the two persons, one of whom has to propose and the other to acknowledge what is called the toast of the evening. On this occasion there is only one exception, because—although I feel at this moment that my knees have refused their natural office, and are more like a pair of castanets than a pair of human supports—I am well aware that I shall be followed by an orator who is known to us all, and to every audience in the United Kingdom. (Applause.) I suppose, gentlemen, that there is not one of us here who has not had the advantage, more than once, of hearing those perplexing orations which Mr. Toole is in the habit of delivering—(laughter) —sublime in execution, yet so complicated and so mysterious—(loud laughter)—in their delivery, that they have often reminded me of what after-dinner speeches of Shakspere's may have been, if we can only imagine that the immortal William was exceedingly drunk at the time. (Laughter.) Well, gentlemen, I have administered to myself the freest dose of compassion for having to propose this illustrious toast this evening, and it has been a problem with me ever since I was asked to fulfil this responsible position why that honour was conferred upon me. A solution of the problem, which has only reached me by a side wind, is that reliable statistics have proved that no young man of my age has ever spent so much money in stalls to see Mr. Toole as I have. (Great applause and laughter.) Gentlemen, that is a reason, and a valid reason; because, when I alluded to his speeches a moment ago, I did not mention them with a view to that Parliamentary success which, I regret to say, has not, on my part, been achieved. I used attentively to attend Mr. Toole's performances, and I have only to mention as a drawback to those who may feel inclined to follow my example, that though you could have heard a pin drop in the house, and though I had read Mill's 'Logic' for hours and hours before going to the theatre, yet when I returned home and attempted to draw up an abstract of the speech I had heard, it was not so clear—(laughter)—or so logical as I should have expected from so eminent a man. (Renewed laughter.) There were brilliant epigrams, and brilliant metaphors, no doubt, but when you came to put epigrams and metaphors together, according to the rules of Mill and Aldrich, you found there was the third premise wanting, which no human ingenuity could supply. (Laughter.) Well, gentlemen, there is another reason why, perhaps, I was chosen chairman on this occasion, and that is on account of a local feeling that I have. I come from the neighbourhood of Edinburgh and I am proud to say, on behalf of Edinburgh, that I believe in that place—in that city—Mr. Toole's first successes were won ; and Edinburgh, I can testify to it, is at this moment an attentive witness of his triumph. Well, gentlemen, if I was to proceed to find fault with the chairman of the dinner, I could do so in a very few words.   I must say that it is impossible that I can do justice to my admirable and honoured friend in any after-remarks I may now choose to make. Steadfast and true as has been his character in every walk of private life, his public career has been so various and so complex that one cannot touch upon all the incidents in one evening's sitting.   I should like to see a series of banquets given day after day in his honour until we had exhausted all the various phases of his character.   Still, although that might redound to his immortal glory, I am doubtful whether it would not result in his precipitate death from indigestion. (Laughter.)   I should like to see a banquet on the first day at which the Lord Chancellor should preside, and at which the

Judges and the Bar of England should be present,
to give their professional and legal opinion as to
the merits of ' Mr. Hammond Coote' and ' Mr.
Serjeant Buzfuz.' (Laughter.) On the second
evening I should like to have a dinner over which
Admiral Rous should be the chairman, and George
Fordham the croupier, and they should give an
opinion as to the merits of Mr. Toole in the pig-
skin (laughter) : and on the third occasion I should
like to have light refreshment, with the members
of both houses of Convocation, the entire bench of
Bishops, and the great clerical dignitaries present,
to dilate upon the manner in which Mr. Toole had
reformed the rogue ' Don Giovanni' by transform-
ing him into a pusillanimous and harmless young
man. (Renewed laughter.) Well, gentlemen, I
am not a dramatic critic, but I can give you in a
very few words the result of my experience. I
have often been to see Mr. Toole, as I said before,
and whenever I have been to see him I have
always entered the house with a feeling of discon-
tent, grumbling to myself that I was perfectly
certain he would not be so good as he was the
last time I saw him, but I have always left the
house with the feeling that I had never seen him
half so good in my life. I cannot account for
that. Then there is another feeling which has
been felt by every human being who has seen him,

whether in town or the provinces, that whenever he has seen Mr. Toole he has not only spent a delightful evening, that he has not only seen an actor of undeniable talent, but that he has met an admirable friend, because there is a geniality about his performance which spreads an electric chain round about his audience, and makes them forget the actor in the friend. (Applause.) Gentlemen, you will read in the third volume of a book recently published a very curious account of how an illustrious man who has passed away from us but recently—I mean the late Charles Dickens—went down to Walworth at some personal inconvenience to see the beginning of a new actor. Dickens admitted that he showed some promise, and he wished to encourage him by his presence and patronage, and that actor, gentlemen, was our guest of this evening. (Cheers.) I cannot help thinking that, if that great genius, Dickens, were able to revisit for a day the scene of his early triumphs, he would think it not the least of his successes in this world that he had introduced us partially to an actor who had been the means of evoking so much happiness and so much sympathy in this country. (Cheers.) We have seen the beginning, but we have not seen the end. We see here a man who has not yet reached the summit of his prosperous career. Well, gentlemen, I will not intrude upon you any longer with my remarks. I have to arraign Mr. Toole on three counts, but I will not interpose longer than I can help between the jury and the counsel for the defence. I have to arraign him on the possession of admirable talents. (Applause.) I have to arraign him also on having conferred more happiness upon his fellow-men, probably, than any human being in this room ; of having made us all his friends, and of possessing the irresistible power of creative sympathy. I have only one word more to say, and that is an allusion to an anecdote that I heard of our guest only the other day. He was told that a few friends would like to give him a dinner before he went to America. To which our illustrious guest replied in a manner that I am perfectly certain you can all figure to yourselves, though I cannot imitate it, ' Why do they want to give me a dinner ? I am not in the least hungry.' (Laughter.) I can understand that remark if Mr. Toole's appetite was one for public applause, because it must have been long ago satisfied. But I should like to tell him, in the presence of this company, why it is we have given him this dinner to-night. We have given it to you, Mr. Toole, because we appreciate the humour which is always genial, and which is always pure (cheers), because we are grateful to you for the many happy evenings we have spent in your presence ; because we feel that that humour is one which is grateful alike to age, and to youth, and to childhood—to the genius and to the fool, to every class and variety and condition of life. We might have felt this equally, and simply waited for stalls to go and realize it in our own persons ; but we wished further to give you this dinner because we feel that we are about to lose you. We are about to lose one who is a household delight of England, and has done more to charm the nation than probably any one man now living ; and, to paraphrase a famous writer, the harmless gaiety of nations is about for the time to be eclipsed. If we have to spare you at all we would rather spare you to our cousins across the Atlantic than to any other nation upon earth. (Applause.) It would be difficult for any Englishman to obtain a cold welcome in America. (Cheers.) What we have to fear for you is not that cold welcome, but that American enthusiasm may induce you for a moment to forget English applause ; and we can only express the hope—and what cheers and repays the encouragement of that hope will be the greatest reward you can give us for our homage to-night —we can only express the hope that American enthusiasm will not make you forget English devotion of many years, and that though you may

leave your new acquaintances with reluctance—
and I have no doubt you will—you will return to
this old country with some pleasure, remembering
that you leave here a nation of friends, to whom
we trust you may be spared for many years to
afford new delight. (Applause.) I will now only
ask the company to drink your very good health,
and may God speed you on a happy and prosperous voyage." (Great cheering.)

Mr. Toole then rose to reply, and on doing so
the whole company also rose, cheered, and waved
their handkerchiefs. This lasted for some minutes.
When the company had resumed their seats, Mr.
Toole said :—" My Lord Rosebery and Gentlemen.
When I look around upon this brilliant company
of men, eminent in science, literature, and art—
men whose names are known wherever the
English language is spoken, and find myself the
guest of so distinguished an assembly, and
with your lordship's generous and flattering
words, together with the gracious message of
H.R.H. the Prince of Wales, fresh in my ears, I
fear lest I should fail to convey the deep sense
of gratitude I must ever entertain for the honour
conferred upon me to-night. You will, I am sure,
forgive me if I add that with my gratitude there
is associated no small amount of honest pride,
because in the compliment now paid to me I

recognize the estimation in which you hold the profession to which I have the honour to belong. While I desire thus publicly and emphatically to acknowledge the kind and generous appreciation that has been extended to me throughout my career, I trust that I shall ever continue to be guided by that principle which I have endeavoured to adopt as the rule of my professional life—faithfulness in my calling as a servant of the public. And suffer me here, also, in a single word, to refer to those happy relations it has ever been my good fortune to maintain with my professional brethren—or shall I say my playmates? Remembering, as I now do, the years of pleasant association with them, I wish, on this, to me memorable, occasion, when I am parting from them for a time, to express the hope that the bond of mutual kindly feeling which has so long existed between us may remain unbroken. Nor must I forget to acknowledge with like gratitude those other equally dear, if more private, relations that may exist between friends of years, so many of whom I recognize here to-night, uniting in that tribute of affectionate regard of which I am so deeply sensible. Some of these friends who see my hands full of home work, have expressed surprise at my quitting England, even for a time. To those friends I have said, what I would now repeat here, that various motives induce me to cross the Atlantic. First and strongest, I frankly admit, is the ambition to win, as an English actor, the approbation of the American playgoing public. The New World has sent to us artists of the highest rank and reputation, ladies and gentlemen who have deservedly achieved distinction in their art. For instance, Miss Cushman, Miss Bateman, Mr. Jefferson, Mr. Sothern, Mr. Owens, Mr. Davenport, Mr. John Brougham, Mr. Edwin Booth, Barney Williams, and many others. Now, if in return I am able to contribute in the smallest degree to the amusement of our American cousins, I shall be well contented. Again, while desirous of avoiding anything like a gloomy view of my visit, I shall yet hope, on my return, to be able ·to render a good dollarous—(laughter and applause)—account. It has been my happy lot to be singularly blessed with the best of health, through which inestimable blessing, during a period of twenty years, I have been enabled to fulfil every performance for which I have been announced, and for which I am truly grateful. On one occasion I was nearly not doing so from a sudden attack of gout, and I sent word to the theatre I was placed *hors de combat*. While I was debating how it was possible for me to go through the performance the manager arrived, and he hobbled into my room, saying I must come down to the theatre at all hazards. He had the gout, and persuaded me it was better for all of us to ' gout ' (go out) together, which we did. (Laughter and applause.) I performed that evening, and was highly complimented on the thoughtful, cautious manner in which I ascended the steps of Uncle Dick's cart. (Laughter.) All this occupation has, of course, made my holidays very occasional ones. When I have had them, my delight has been to spend them at the theatre as an auditor. Two of these occasions have occurred during my last season in London, which I remember with great pleasure. The first was spent in the stalls of the Gaiety Theatre, in witnessing the ever-fresh, polished, and exquisite acting of my old—though ever young—friend, Charles Mathews —(loud cheers)—the second time I went to the Lyceum, and wept over the woes of ' Charles the First,' so admirably and artistically portrayed by my good friend Henry Irving—(loud cheers)—and the enjoyment I experienced on both those occasions gave me a longing desire for more holidays. But, my Lord Rosebery and gentlemen, I must not further occupy your time, for however ready I may be in giving utterance to the words of others, I feel my power of expression on such an occasion as this to be very feeble indeed. Once more I thank you heartily—very, very heartily. That your good wishes go with me I know; that my earnest gratitude is yours you will, I am sure, believe. Deeply and sincerely I thank you, one and all, for the high and flattering compliment you have been pleased to pay me to-night, a compliment which will never quit my memory, however sorely it may be tried—a compliment which will ever mark one of the pleasantest episodes in my not altogether uneventful life. Permit me, then, my lord and gentlemen, with a heart more full than the glass I now hold, to drink to your hearty good health, and your greatest happiness."

The conclusion of this speech was the signal for another loud and prolonged outburst of applause.

Mr. Douglas Straight proposed " Literature and Art," to which Mr. Edmund Yates replied for " Literature," and Mr. W. R. Frith, R.A., for " Art." Mr. E. J. Reed gave " The Health of the Chairman," who, having responded, called upon Mr. Charles Mathews to propose " The Drama."

Mr. Mathews said:—"My Lord and Gentlemen, I really consider that I have been called upon very suddenly for this toast. I certainly thought that if I had been required to speak you would have had a song first in order to give me time to prepare. My extemporaneous speeches are always the better for a little preparation. (Laugh-

ter.)   I finished work last night, and I thought
I was going to enjoy myself here as a
private gentleman this evening, but it seems to
me that I am not to be permitted to do so.   I am
called upon to propose 'The Drama,' though why
I should be called upon to propose it I do not
know.   Certainly, I have been acquainted with
the drama for some years—(laughter)—a sort of
distant connection—a sort of bowing acquaintance
—but really I cannot do justice to its beauties.   I
should just as soon think of raking up the ashes
of my deceased grandfather for the purpose of in-
voking his aid.   Besides, I do not see what the
drama has to do with Mr. Toole's success in
America.   (Laughter.)   It is not the drama that
is going to America ; it is Mr. Toole—(laughter)
—and I have heard several gentlemen say all his
pieces have been played to death in America.
That is the greatest mistake.   Mr. Toole will
bring them to life again.   The people do not go
to the theatre to see the pieces ; they go to see
Mr. Toole.   He is the speciality, the type.   They
do not care about the author any more than does
Mr. Toole himself.   (Cheers and laughter.)   And
I advise Mr. Toole, although he has quoted Shakspere this evening, not to follow it up by coming
out in Shaksperian drama in America.   Perhaps
they might expect to have the right words, though

if Mr. Toole did give them Shakspere according to
Toole they might not find it out, for a great many
people talk of Shakspere who have not read him.
(Cheers.)   However, I can tell Mr. Toole he will
have a jolly time of it, and I wish I was going
with him.   I will now address myself to him personally.   If you stop too long, who knows but
that I may take up some of your parts ? (Laughter.)   That you will see when you come back.
I certainly shall not take to the Shaksperian
drama.   During the last forty years I do not think
I have read forty lines of blank verse, and I do
not suppose I shall for the next forty years.   I
think we had better connect this toast with the
American drama, and then he can tell them out
there that we did so, and they will say, ' Bravo,
Toole.'   (Laughter.)   You know we have one
drama coming out now by an American author,
Dion Boucicault.   (Great laughter.)   As Mr.
Benjamin Webster has slipped out of harness, I
will connect this toast with the name of Mr.
Creswick." [2]   (Cheers.)

[2] Mr. William Creswick died on Sunday, June 17th, 1888,
at his residence, The Terrace, Kennington Park, London.
The following details of his career are compiled from the *Era*
and other authorities :—" Born on the 27th of December, 1813,
in the vicinity of Covent Garden, Mr. Creswick was in the
habit of seeing as a boy the most eminent performers attached
to the neighbouring theatres.   Although educated for a mercan-

Mr. Creswick having responded, Mr. Charles Dickens, jun., proposed as a last toast, " The

tile pursuit, he soon evinced a decided predilection for the stage. At the age of seventeen his home was broken up by the death of his father, and he felt free to follow his inclinations. In the summer of 1831 he accepted an engagement at a small theatre in the Commercial Road, of which Amherst, of Astley's, was manager. Here was produced a drama founded on the murder of the Italian boy ' burked ' for purposes of dissection, and, under the name of Master Collins, the youthful actor impersonated the victim of the atrocious crime, which was then creating a painful sensation throughout the country. Soon after he joined a small company of players in Suffolk, with whom he remained two years, and afterwards rose to a better position in the Kentish circuit of Mr. John Sloman. In 1834 he was playing leading business in Downe's well-managed York circuit, where he met Miss Paget, of the Olympic Theatre, destined to become Mrs. Creswick ; whilst the company also included Henry Compton, John Ryder, and Harry Widdicomb, all then in their novitiate. Returning to London, Mr. Creswick made his first prominent appearance, February 16th, 1835, as ' Horace Meredith,' in Jerrold's comedy of *The School-fellows*, at the old Queen's Theatre, in Tottenham Street, Tottenham Court Road, placed at the time under the management of Mrs. Nisbett. Going back to York circuit, Mr. Creswick embodied the leading part in Talfourd's tragedy of *Ion*, then played in the provinces for the first time. In April, 1839, the Lyceum was opened by Mr. Penley, a provincial manager, with three new pieces—a drama called *Lady Mary Wortley Montagu*, of which Mrs. Stirling was the heroine, a farce called *Dark Deeds*, and a melodrama entitled *The Silver Crescent*. of which Mr. Edward Stirling was the author. In the course of a few nights the manager hit upon the odd expedient of throwing open the stage to the audience at the end of the second piece and giving a promenade concert. Every effort, however, proved fruitless, the season abruptly concluded

Press," which was acknowledged by Mr. G. A. Sala. Some pleasant music during the evening was

after a fortnight, and an excellent company, which included Mr. Creswick, was suddenly dispersed, as they declined to continue on the sharing system. Mr. Creswick then made a professional tour through America and Canada, where he remained nearly four years, greatly increasing his reputation. Returning to England, he played as a tragedian at Newcastle-on-Tyne, Liverpool, and Birmingham ; finally, in July, 1846, joining Mr. Samuel Phelps at Sadler's Wells, where he made his first appearance as ' Hotspur ' in *Henry IV.* In April, 1847, when Mrs. Fanny Kemble Butler reappeared on the stage at the Princess's, Mr. Creswick was engaged to support her, and he then played with Macready, who was giving a series of farewell performances previous to his departure for America. This was followed by a three years' engagement at the Haymarket where he opened as ' Claude ' to the ' Pauline ' of Miss Helen Faucit. In the autumn of 1849 Mr. Creswick joined Mr. Shepherd in the management of the Surrey, opening as ' Alasco ' in Sheridan Knowles's play of *The Rose of Arragon*, and for three years afterwards playing a round of Shaksperian characters. In September, 1866, Mr. Shepherd had again a partnership with Mr. Creswick at the Surrey, and the T. P. Cooke prize drama *True to the Core*, in which Mr. Creswick played ' Martin Truegold ' was produced on the opening night of the season. A second visit was paid to America in 1871, when he acted at Boston with Charlotte Cushman and Edwin Booth. Returning to England, Mr. Creswick appeared with Samuel Phelps at Drury Lane Theatre, and remained some time. A benefit performance was given him at the Gaiety in May, 1877, when he played ' Macbeth,' and shortly afterwards left for Australia, where he was enthusiastically welcomed. Returning from his triumphant tour, Mr. Creswick reappeared at the Surrey in his favourite character of ' Virginius,' and played starring engagements at the Standard and other theatres. In November, 1882, he took a ' Jubilee presided over by Sir Julius Benedict, the vocalists who gave their services being Miss Rose Hersee, Miss Alice Fairman, Miss A. Pulham, Mr. George Fox, Mr. W. Righton, and Mr. G. Perren ; Mr. Henry Lazarus giving a solo on the clarionet.

The following is a list of the company present :—

Capt. J. E. F. Aylmer.
James Albery, Esq.
H. L. Bateman, Esq.
J. Benjamin, Esq.
B. Bethell, Esq.
J. Bidwell, Esq.
John Billington, Esq.
E. Boyle, Esq.
H. J. Byron, Esq.
Sir Julius Benedict.
Lieut.-Col. Brabazon.
Hon. E. Balfour.
W. E. Bevan, Esq.
J. Batchelor, Esq.
Peter Berlyn, Esq.
T. J. Bishop, Esq.
W. Barlow, Esq.
W. Burton, Esq.
H. Bayley, Esq.
E. J. Beale, Esq.
Rev. J. E. Cox.
William Creswick, Esq.
James Carey, Esq.

Charles Coote, Esq.
E. W. Cathie, Esq.
R. M. Curtis, Esq.
William Day, Esq.
Charles Dickens, Esq.
J. Dennistoun, Esq.
J. Drew, Esq.
H. Evill, Esq.
W. P. Frith, Esq., R.A.
Lieut.-Col. Farquharson.
G. Farquhar, Esq.
Horace Farquhar, Esq.
G. Fox, Esq.
J. H. Fyfe, Esq.
J. A. Gilbert, Esq.
W. S. Gilbert, Esq.
F. Herbert, Esq.
C. Harris, Esq.
Dr. Harper.
J. M. Hart, Esq.
J. Hilton, Esq., F.R.S.
N. A. Hunt, Esq.
Henry Irving, Esq.

Benefit,' under the auspices of Mr. Henry Irving, at the Lyceum Theatre ; and on October 29th, 1885, a complimentary benefit was given to the esteemed actor at Drury Lane Theatre, when he appeared in a scene from *King Lear* (act i. scene 3), and took his farewell of the stage.

J. Jeffrey, Esq.
David James, Esq.
Dr. F. C. Jones.
F. Knollys, Esq.
Henry Lee, Esq.
Albert Levy, Esq.
Edward Ledger, Esq.
E. Lowne, Esq.
M. D. Longden, Esq.
G. J. Leon, Esq.
H. Lazarus, Esq.
G. Loveday, Esq.
C. J. Mathews, Esq.
W. F. Maitland, Esq.
A. Montgomery, Esq.
Frank Marshall, Esq.
Isaac Mead, Esq.
John Oxenford, Esq.
Dr. O'Connor.
G. Offor, Esq.
Lord Alfred Paget.
J. C. Pawle, Esq.
George Perren, Esq.
G. F. Pinches, Esq.
C. F. Partington, Esq.
H. B. Pritchard, Esq.
G. Painter, Esq.
Dr. R. Quain, F.R.S.
E. J. Reed, Esq., M.P.
Robert Reece, Esq.
Colonel Richards.
H. Roberts, Esq.
E. Routledge, Esq.
J. Sargent, Esq.

Sir Bruce Seton.
Barry Sullivan, Esq.
W. Stevens, Esq.
G. A. Sala, Esq.
Douglas Straight, Esq.
Charles Shaw, Esq.
J. Ashby Sterry, Esq.
J. Early Smith, Esq.
J. Smith, Esq.
J. Saunders, Esq.
Reeves Smith, Esq.'
Samuel L. Schuster, Esq.
Rev. F. F. Statham, B.A.
Arthur Stirling, Esq.
Rev. Dr. Tisdale.
E. W. Tritton, Esq.
J. Taylor, Esq.
W. Tinsley, Esq.
A. Thompson, Esq.
T. J. Thompson, Esq.
Frank F. Toole, Esq.
F. C. Toole, Esq.
J. L. Toole, jun., Esq.
E. Trimmer, Esq.
Thomas Thorne, Esq.
E. J. Tomson, Esq.
James Vicars, Esq.
Benjamin Webster, Esq.
Alfred Wigan, Esq.
W. T. Wrighton, Esq.
Hon. L. Wingfield.
Alderman Sir T. White.
T. Webb, Esq.
Edmund Yates, Esq.

III.

THE farewell dinner given to Mr. Toole at Bir-

mingham took place at the Great Western Hotel,
Mr. George Dawson [3] presiding; Mr. Samuel Tim-

MR. GEORGE DAWSON.

mins occupying the vice-chair.   Sixty friends and
admirers of the popular comedian were present,

[3] George Dawson, lecturer, preacher, and journalist, was
born in St. Pancras, London, 1821, but lived most of his life
in Birmingham, where he was deservedly esteemed as an
honest and earnest social and political reformer.   He took
the degree of M.A. at the University of Glasgow, and was
intended for the ministry of the Baptist Nonconformists.   In
this capacity he became minister of Mount Zion Chapel at
Birmingham.   "The peculiarities of his ministrations," says

including Alderman Biggs, Alderman Cornforth, Councillor Barrett, Dr. Wade, Major Gem, Capt. Bullock, Dr. Suffield, Messrs. Mercer, Simpson,

a brief biography in " Men of the Time " for 1872, "and chiefly a disregard of the merely conventional usages of the sacred office alienated from him a portion of the congregation of Mount Zion Chapel, and a separation took place, when the majority seceded with the minister. A subscription was immediately commenced for the erection of a new chapel for Mr. Dawson, and in 1847 the edifice was opened as the Church of the Saviour. Mr. Dawson did not advocate peculiarities of doctrine, but rather made an earnest desire for truth, and a life of obedience to God and charity to man, the great test of a Christian spirit." Mr. Dawson was an intimate friend of Mr. Henry Barnett, who for some years was the preacher at Finsbury Chapel (succeeding Mr. Fox, M.P.), and at the same time editor of the *Sunday Times*, Barnet being a Conservative in politics and Dawson a Liberal. Mr. Dawson was better known as a lecturer than as a preacher, and since his death many of his public addresses have been published in one or two volumes, admirable examples of literary and oratorical art. He wrote for the *Birmingham Daily Press*, a journal of which he was part proprietor, and in which enterprise he lost money. He was not fortunate in his journalistic career. He started the *Birmingham Morning News*, which, in spite of his strong hand in the editorial columns, did not make its way financially. In this instance the capitalist was a wealthy Manchester man. Mr. Dawson for many years took an active part in the public life of Birmingham, was a member of the School Board, delivered inaugural addresses at the beginnings of several public institutions, took great interest in the foundation of the Free Reference and the Shakspere Libraries, and was beloved of all classes in the Midland metropolis, where a public monument has been erected to his memory.

James Rodgers, Yeoville Thomason, J. Harding,
G. Wilkinson, E. Pickering, W. Lyndon, Thomas
Ingram, F. Badham, Baron Clive, R. Free, J.
Machin, H. Bennett, T. N. Brown, W. H. Ward,
J. Hollingsworth, J. Ward, G. Loveday, R. Best,
J. Knight, R. Thomas, G. Baker, J. Lampard,
W. Latham, Oscar Pollock, &c., &c.   The ar-
rangements for the dinner were admirably carried
out by the committee, Messrs. W. J. Ward, J.
Rodgers, and J. Hollingsworth.

The Chairman, proposing the toast of the evening, "Our Guest," said :—" Before I propose the
toast which it is my honour and pleasure to
propose, I have to say that some gentlemen, who
appear to have been at Willis's Rooms on a recent
occasion, telegraph : 'London fills yet another
sparkling bumper, asking, as a postscript from
Willis's, to unite with Birmingham at five o'clock
in hearty good wishes to the Prince of Wales of
comedians, the amiable chairman, his virtuous vice,
and to the fraternal company all round.   Hoping all
are in a merry key, JOHN BULL, No. 1, London.'
(Laughter.)   I propose the health of our guest—
(applause)—and in doing so I have a great deal
of pleasure, because there are foolish people who
are willing to be amused and are willing to forget
those who amuse them.   That is a form of ingrati-
tude of which I am not capable.   If a man who

made a doll for my little child were to come to me
and say he was the dollmaker to my little child, I
should honour him much for having given innocent
pleasure to an innocent child; and if, later on—
when pleasure is harder to be got, and therefore
the more precious, because of its scarcity and difficulty—if there is a man who can give any number
of us innocent pleasure and intellectual gratifica-
tion, he deserves thanks and honour, and I have
often felt very indignant at those who go to be
entertained and amused, and then go away and
slight those who have entertained and amused
them. (Applause.) If I were ashamed to be
president here to-day, I should be ashamed to have
ever laughed at Mr. Toole. (Hear, hear.) He
has conquered my habitual gravity more than
once—(laughter)—and put my solemnity to rout
in the most shameless manner. I feel indebted to
him for doing so, and I am glad of this humble
means of in part paying the debt I owe him.
Were I given to require the shelter of great names
for what I do, I need hardly tell you we could put
our fingers on numbers, but I will only refer to
Samuel Johnson, who, respecting Garrick, formerly
his pupil, wrote one of the sweetest of all epitaphs
—'The death of Garrick has eclipsed the gaiety
of nations.' If I were to say—not the death—but
the partial retirement of Mr. Toole had eclipsed

the gaiety of nations I should err, for he goes to conquer the gravity of another nation as he has conquered the gravity of this. (Applause.) I have no doubt he will have as much success there as he has had here. (Hear, hear.) I would not retail his little point, nor do I wish to spoil his little joke; but I do hope that his 'dollarous campaign' on the other side of the water may be equal to his 'sovereign progress' in this country. (Laughter and applause.) I have to congratulate Mr. Toole upon his courage. I know he is not one of those rash mortals who would go to sea if nobody had been before. (Laughter.) I know it is his weak point; he confesses it, and I hope he will have a very quiet passage, as I am certain he will have a very hearty welcome. (Hear, hear.) And should he be prostrate, he must comfort himself with the thought of the hearty friends he has left behind and is about to make, and I have this pleasure to hold out to him, that very soon after he lands in New York he and I have agreed to dine together—(hear, hear)—and then I shall be able to administer any ghostly consolation of which he may stand in need. (Laughter.) I need not say we go on different errands; but we go very much in the same spirit. (Applause.) And if our going, humble people as we are—if we should do anything, even by one thread, to knit together these two great nations—for it must be remembered when Gulliver was bound in Lilliput, each thread was a very flimsy one, but the great multitude of them made them strong—therefore, however fine the line we may spin, we may hope that the many which have been, and the many which will be, may help to prevent the greatest of all possible scandals, the saddest of all possible injuries—discord between the two great nations which speak the same tongue. (Applause.) No doubt Mr. Toole will find, as I shall, that it seems a very strange thing to be in another country where our own tongue is spoken. Mr. Toole speaks French like a native—(laughter)—of France—(renewed laughter)—but the strangeness of being in a country politically different, but where the language spoken is the same as our own, will give him and myself a more interesting view of the history of the last hundred years. I shall be able to tell you how he behaves himself, and he will be able to report upon me—(laughter)—though I am afraid I shall go to see him far oftener than he will come to see me. In saying this I mean no reproach, for I have seen Mr. Toole on Sunday—to use an old phrase—'sitting under me.' (Laughter.) I have seen him reverent, devout, and attentive, and I have sometimes thought I have done him some little good. I know he has

done me a great deal of good, for he has made me enjoy the quainter scenes of one side of human nature, and I hope I have done something to show how deeply rooted to the greater and nobler part of human nature are those things he deals in. (Hear, hear.) I wish him great success. We know he will not desert the country of his birth, or become a naturalized citizen of America, but will come back, and we shall have, I hope, the pleasure of welcoming him. (Hear, hear.) I propose that we drink very heartily his health. We drink it not only because he is an artist, but because he is—as I have known him—in private life an upright, honourable, hospitable, generous, merciful, and kindly man. (Applause.) These things I know, and therefore, when I propose his health, he knows, and some of you know, that it is not a mere matter of form ; I do it with all my heart, he being as honourable a man as a private gentleman as he is admirable artist as an actor."
(Loud applause.)

The toast having been enthusiastically honoured, Mr. Toole said :—" I thank you very much and very heartily for the very kind way in which you have responded to the toast so kindly proposed by my friend Mr. Dawson. I am a very poor speaker—(laughter)—but I may say I esteem this meeting a very high compliment. It is the last before I go, and I appreciate it the more because of the sacrifice which some of the gentlemen present have had to make to be present on a Saturday afternoon. However, you have kindly considered my professional duties, and I thank you heartily. I was once very severely rebuked by an old lady who was interviewing—that is an Americanism, I suppose I must get used to Americanism—(laughter)—who was interviewing my wife at a party. She asked my wife whether she went to the theatre. 'Yes, when there is a new piece on,' replied she. 'I suppose your husband goes,' said the old lady. 'Oh, yes, he goes every evening,' replied my wife. 'Lord bless me, how gay he must be!' said the horrified old lady. (Laughter.) It is very gratifying to me to have my health proposed by so eloquent and distinguished a gentleman as Mr. George Dawson. He has spoken of my going to hear him, and I may say that going to hear him is one of my great delights in coming to Birmingham. I enjoy nothing more than hearing Mr. Dawson in his own church. (Hear, hear.) I find him a gentleman able to vastly and powerfully impress me. We meet him as a natural gentleman, and we have a natural discourse which does us good. I confess I do not like to be very much frightened at church, neither do I think that sort of thing does much good—(hear, hear, and laughter)—but when we learn to love and honour the peacher, a discourse such as Mr. Dawson's is of eminent service to us. (Hear, hear.) Mr. Dawson has given me a promise to dine with me in New York.[1]   Well, I shall arrive there a fortnight

---

[1] There are several notes in these volumes which Mr. Toole will probably not see until they are in the hands of the public, and this is one of them. It refers to the many special acts of charity and benevolence which have been mentioned to the chronicler by various correspondents. Some of the letters are from children, others are from secretaries of public institutions, and one or two are from men of an entirely private station. They are all full of gratitude for the help Mr. Toole has given to "those who are in necessity and tribulation." One corre-spondent draws special attention to the liberal and broad spirit in which Mr. Toole helps deserving charities either with his purse or his time. Mr. Toole is a member of the Church of England, but his sympathies are with the charities of every denomination of religionists, and he is tolerant of every creed. From a heap of correspondence of this class the chronicler selects for publication a note from Mr. Ralph Harrison, for-merly manager of the *Birmingham Daily Gazette.* "Shortly before J. L. Toole's departure for America," writes Mr. Harrison, "he was fulfilling an engagement at Birmingham. At the time there was a bazaar for the benefit of Roman Catholic Schools being held in the Town Hall. There were few visitors at the hall, and the whole affair was likely to be a miserable failure, when a gentleman suggested to the manager of the bazaar that if Toole could be got to sing a song or two, he might draw an audience. The manager rubbed his hands with delight at the idea, and the gentleman undertook to see Mr. Toole on the subject. 'Certainly,' said Toole, who added, 'I shall come with plea-

before him, and I shall be able to crow over him like a native—(laughter)—and I'll show him round. (Renewed laughter.) Possibly he may meet with some odd things in the course of his rambles, and if he becomes President, which I think very likely—(laughter)—I shall knock at the door and say, ' I want to see the President,' and I will remind him of having been in the chair to-day. (Laughter.) And if, when we return 1000*l.* is wanted for any of the Birmingham hospitals—I have an ambition to play Shakspere

sure.' Toole's resolve was intimated to the bazaar manager, who immediately got large posters printed, announcing ' J. L. Toole at the Town Hall to-morrow at 12.' When to-morrow came there was quite a rush, and the large Town Hall was crammed by twelve o'clock. Toole came and brought John Maclean with him, and the two together amused and interested the immense audience for nearly an hour, Toole singing some of his favourite songs and John Maclean reciting ' The Bridge of Sighs,' and other popular pieces. Both actors were loudly cheered, and Toole, before leaving, invested something like 5*l.* on bazaar odds and ends. But this was not all ; Toole told the manager to announce him again for the night, and between the pieces at the Prince of Wales's Theatre he took a cab and drove down to the Town Hall and gave another immense audience two songs, for which he was rapturously encored. Toole then made his way back to the theatre to play in *Ici on Parle Français.* And so what was like to be a complete failure of a bazaar was, by the kindness of the great comedian and his friend Maclean, turned into an enormous success, and the Roman Catholic Institute was greatly benefited by the proceeds."

—I will play the principal gravedigger, but only to Mr. Dawson's ' Hamlet '—(laughter)—for I am sure he could act. (Renewed laughter.) I should like to retire on the proceeds. (Laughter.) And I would promise him the same thing should not be repeated which once occurred when I played the gravedigger to Mr. T. C. King. Unfortunately, the stage was rather small and the box was rather large, and I dropped the skull to the bottom. Of course the soliloquy could not go on ; the gallery boys were rather indignant, and one shouted, ' Come out, Toole, and give us a song ! ' (Laughter.) I must again thank you very sincerely for the great compliment you have paid me. I have had the good fortune to spend very many happy days in Birmingham, but this will be remembered as one of the happiest. It is a great pleasure for me to see one of my oldest friends in Birmingham in the vice-chair, and to see present the two managers of the theatres, who have behaved so handsomely and courteously to me. I wish I could say a great deal more, but you must not measure the depth of my gratitude by the very imperfect words I have given utterance to. As Jim Brass says, ' He was not a good speaker, but he was a deep thinker,' and I shall think deeply of this very happy gathering all through my tour. Permit me to wish you all good health, long life, and happiness." (Loud applause.)

Mr. Alderman Cornforth proposed "The Drama," and Captain Bullock "Our Theatres," to which Mr. Mercer Simpson and Mr. Rogers replied, the latter gentleman, in conclusion, giving "The Health of the Chairman," a gentleman, he said, who threw off the narrow trammels of bigotry, and came amongst them, actors and managers, on all occasions in the belief that they were reasonable, rational, and intellectual beings, and that their mission and their pleasure was not to demoralize the public, but to elevate it by healthy, wholesome, and instructive amusement. It was a matter of great congratulation to find a reverend gentleman of Mr. Dawson's high character and culture sitting at the head of that table.

The Chairman, in response, said he made no pretensions to the title "reverend." There were some things which he thought could be said to men and women useful to be said, and they thought he was able to say them, and that was all. He was no priest, no dignitary of the Church. He was not "reverend," but "reverent"—(hear, hear)—and one sign of his being so was his being there, for he reverenced the whole of man's nature, except when it strayed from righteousness and truth. He reverenced the actor who faithfully performed his duty, he reverenced all honest work, all honest men, whatever their calling, the little child, the little dog, all nature. He reverenced man, woman, and child, and he thought he reverenced God. Therefore, though not " reverend," he was " reverent," and he thought that the better word of the two. As to being a " divine "—(laughter)—he was afraid no College of Divines would admit him, but he was content to be thrown out if he were admitted to colleges of men like that. He sincerely thanked them for their heartiness. He was too old to be taken in by appearances. He knew that what Mr. Rogers said he meant, and he knew from their faces they meant it, for one of the chiefest blessings of his life had been that during the whole time he had been in Birmingham, though some had blamed him and differed from him, yet when they had spoken kindly to him, he had felt they meant it. Man, woman, or child, he believed, had never spoken to him kindly without meaning it, and if he achieved no greater honour, no greater blessing, he was content. To have been kindly spoken to, and always from the heart, atoned for many mistakes, for many unpleasantnesses, for crookedness he might have made or run against. Nothing had given him more pleasure in Birmingham than that. (Hear, hear.) So he believed it had been that day, and so might it be until he retired into private life—or into that most private life, to which for a time they must all go—he hoped, to meet again. (Loud applause.)

The company then separated.

II.

IN AMERICA.

Wig and Gown on the stage and off—" Too English "—American independence—The press—Playing at a lunatic asylum—An emotional Scotchman—Fechter—Welcomed at the Lotos—A poem by William Winter—Toole interviewed on his American impressions—First appearance—The next day's criticism—Notes on the American tour—Canada—The story of an editor and his wife—The coming holiday.

I.

" My American tour, which lasted over a year, was in every way successful, and in many ways pleasant. The Americans, when I went over, were not quite ' so English,' as they are now. I opened in Albery's play of *Wig and Gown*, which they didn't understand at all. It was ' too utterly English, you know.' The barrister's wig and gown is not an American institution. Learned gentlemen plead there in ordinary attire, and in some courts with a cigar in their mouths. This seems a little out of keeping with our notions of the dignity of the law ; but I once saw a priest smoking a cigarette in a Continental cathedral and, after all, that is even still more opposed to our prejudices. There is no harm, of course, in either case. Nothing is wrong, I suppose, unless you mean it to be ; and justice, I daresay, can be

MR. TOOLE IN "OFF THE LINE."

obtained as well without a wig as with it. I had to withdraw *Wig and Gown* after trying it for a week, though some of the scenes which the audiences did understand went capitally.

"*Off the Line, Dearer than Life, Oliver Twist Paul Pry, Dot,* were the pieces that pleased the Americans most ; and the leading New York papers were unanimous in their complimentary notices.

"I received many kindly tributes from both actors and playgoers, was frequently interviewed, had pleasant dinners given me here and there, and a most kindly reception at the Lotos Club. I went to Long Branch, and sprained my ankle— an accident which a minor critic, who, I suppose, had been somewhat haughtily treated by George Loveday, declared was an advertisement. The doctors said it was a sprain, and I know it pained me a good deal, which would not have been the case if it had been an advertisement.

"I travelled right through the States with varying fortune, but nowhere without receiving much kindness, nowhere without enthusiastic audiences.

"Theatres have very much improved within the last dozen years, not only in America, but in England, though I do not remember any house more primitive in England than one at which I played out West. There was a balcony in front of the theatre, with a band of music which played outside, after the manner of Richardson's Show at Greenwich Fair when I was a boy.

" In some cities the critics—who, by the way, were invariably kindly—thought I was too English; and at Boston, in a little speech which I made at the close of my engagement there after several very cordial calls, I told them that I was English, that my plays were English, and that I acted in English, and felt sure they would have been surprised if I had played to them in Italian, in German, or in Dutch. When Mr. Jefferson came to England we knew that he was an American, and we expected him to be national; and he was, and very delighted we were with his art. I thanked the American people for their welcome, and for their acknowledgment of the truth they found in my interpretations of Dickens."

" What about your audiences ? " I suggested.

" As a rule," he replied, " sympathetic and enthusiastic. They varied. What pleased them especially in one city was the thing they cared less about in another. I sometimes think one city made a point, as a matter of independence, of not liking what another went mad about. At the same time there was not an audience anywhere that I didn't feel I touched deeply in ' Michael Garner ' and ' Caleb Plummer.' And the longer I stayed in a town the larger my audiences grew, and the more the number of my friends increased."

" You enjoyed your trip ? "

" Very much. So also did my wife. My daughter, Florence, remained for some time in New York, where she entered upon a course of study. My son, Frank, travelled with me: the extremes of temperature were rather trying to him, as indeed they were to several members of my company. I felt the over-heating of the railway cars and the hot dressing-rooms now and then as an inconvenience; and I must confess that outside the great cities the food seemed to me to be very inferior and badly cooked. The country impressed me immensely; the splendid ranges of mountains, the great rivers, and the busy, excited, energetic crowds of people in the cities.

" My experiences of the newspapers, on the whole, were very pleasant. My manager, George Loveday, conducted our business on very independent and fearless lines. A few little waspish journals that you know exist here and there didn't relish this. They took it out of us now and then in what George called ' a scorcher ;' but we were English, you know, and kept to our English ways. I don't know whether that was altogether wise, in spite of the proverb, when at Rome, do as the Romans do ; but at least we held our own, made friends, I think, of the best people, and won our way to the respect and esteem of the highest critics.

"Some of our pieces on first representation were a little like olives to unaccustomed palates, and seemed to bother them. 'Spriggins' and the 'Dodger,' essentially London types, although of very opposite characters, puzzled them a good deal; but on return visits they became immense favourites. The characters the Americans didn't quite understand in my *répertoire*, however, went straight home to the Canadians. I felt perfectly at my ease in the Dominion; it was, in fact, England; the theatres English, the audiences English; and there was nothing we played that was not accepted with the same applause and laughter which belonged to my experiences of the United Kingdom.

"I always find it difficult to talk about myself and my acting. I hate to be egotistical, and believe I am naturally modest; but when one has worked very hard and studied all one knows to realize an author's conception of character and to give life to it, of course nothing is more gratifying than the approving voices of big audiences. I had very earnest and complimentary invitations from managers right through the United States and Canada to remain another year, and not a season passes that invitations do not come asking me to name terms for another American tour.

" I gave several entertainments at public institutions in America ; two at the famous Pittsburg Lunatic Asylum at Dick's Pound.   Dr. Reid was the master of the institution, a singularly accomplished and earnest man.   After a miscellaneous programme, concluding with *Off the Line*, he addressed myself and company in one of the most eloquent speeches I ever listened to, referring to the condition of the patients, some of whom were sufficiently capable to have enjoyed intensely the evening's amusement, others who would have vague and curious impressions of it, but for all of whom it represented a certain amount of such intellectual light and mirthfulness as they had the capacity to enjoy.   It would always remain with them ; if somewhat vague, a pleasant impression. A few might take it out into the world in after life ; but with many it would remain with them under that roof until they passed away, for the majority were destined never to go beyond those walls.

" I afterwards received in England an account of the last occasion of my visit to the Asylum, and a very complimentary letter in the Report, which they publish annually as to the work and progress of the institution."

II.

" AT Buffalo, where I played two nights, having hired the theatre from Meach Brothers, I played *Off the Line, Ici, Paul Pry*, and the Dodger scene

THE DODGER AND "THE MAN WHO COULDN'T HELP CRYING."

from *Oliver Twist*. There is a pathetic scene in *Off the Line*. A man during the performance stood at the wings, and was deeply affected. I couldn't help noticing his emotion, so evidently genuine, and, of course, so very complimentary. It would not have escaped the sympathetic eye of Charles Kean, had he been the actor who had inspired it; and I confess this little tribute behind the scenes did not annoy me. But what *did* upset and astonish me very considerably was the fact that when I appeared as the ' Dodger,' the man at the wings not only didn't laugh, but he actually cried. There was no mistake about it, he wept; and when I came off, he mopped his face with his handkerchief, and said, ' Oh, Mr. Toole, you must excuse me, I can't help it; you must remember me years ago; it turned me right over to see those trousers again! I was the wardrobe-keeper at the Theatre Royal, Edinburgh, thirty years ago, when first you played the '' Dodger'' there; my name is Weems; when I saw those trousers, I was reminded of my dear old home in Scotland, and I couldn't have helped crying had it been to save my life.'

'' Among those who had preceded me with my pieces was Beckett, who had taken all my gags and business. This induced some persons to think I was imitating Beckett. Among professionals from whom I received much personal kindness were Warren, the famous Boston comedian, Florence, and Barrett.''

III.

'' The night Irving first played ' Hamlet' in London I was fulfilling an engagement in Philadelphia.

Fechter called and came into my dressing-room.
' I wonder how he will get on,' said Fechter,
thinking no doubt of the sensation he had made in
the part years before.

" Fechter was altogether an altered man since
I had last met him. From an elegant, picturesque

MR. FECHTER.

figure he had become fat and gross. He had
lots of ability, but lacked ballast. A kindly man ;
excitable, could not stand success, couldn't carry
it. He wanted me to go round starring with him
through America in *Robert Macaire*.

" Widdicombe played with Fechter at the

Adelphi. The day before Widdicombe died (he had acted at the Surrey many years, and was a great favourite) I went to see him. There were two men in his bedroom, and just as I went in one of them was saying ' Good-bye.' The second was Creswick. Creswick remained in the room. The window was opposite Widdicombe's bed, and Creswick was in a strong light. The man who left was Fechter : he shook hands with me. I asked Creswick who the stranger was. " Some sporting friend," he replied.

" ' How are you, Widdicombe ? ' I asked.

" ' I am better to-day, dear fellow ; but a little dull, just a trifle below par ; I have been looking at Crezzy's wig—so long known to us—I have seen it so many years—feel a little tired—I think it's the wig.'

" Creswick, as you know, wore the most palpable and aggressive wig ; his head was bald all over. Poor Byron used to call him Creswig.

" Fechter had a farm in Pennsylvania, and lived there in the intervals of his professional tours. He had fifty-seven acres. I understood that he lived a curious kind of life. He married, as a second wife, Miss Lizzie Price, who had supported him in his leading engagements.

" His house was quite a pretty place, I was told, set back from the highway, covered with creepers ;

had handsome plate-glass windows, a grass plot, an old-fashioned pump and well, a nice garden, and in his study there were no end of firearms. He was fond of sport, both shooting and fishing, kept quite a collection of dogs; but all the exercise that this suggests did not overcome his tendency to obesity.

"When I saw him he was an entirely different man from the elegant actor who had drawn the town to the Adelphi. He died at the comparatively early age of fifty-six, having held a prominent position on the stage, not only in England and America, but in France and Germany."

IV.

THE modesty of my friend in regard to his American tour is remarkably illustrated by a collection of Press notices which I have received from Mr. Lowne, who not only delights in amassing all kinds of newspaper records relating to Mr. Toole and Mr. Irving, but who posts up in his scrapbooks from day to day something like a history of the world. I am indebted to Mr. Lowne for the loan of several of these volumes, which have enabled me now and then to assist my host's memory, and from which I venture to make a few extracts relating to Mr. Toole's American tour, and his impressions of the United States.

His reception at the Lotos Club was of a very flattering character. Some seventy-five guests attended, among whom were Mr. Floyd, of Wallack's Theatre, the representative of Mr. John Lester Wallack, who was detained by

MR. WILLIAM WINTER.

illness ; Mr. Augustin Daly, of the Fifth Avenue Theatre : Mr. John T. Ford, manager of Baltimore and Washington Theatres ; Mr. William Stuart, Joseph Jefferson, Charles Gayler, John T. Raymond, John McCulloch, Charles Brookes, W. S. Andrews, and a large number of actors and lovers of the drama. Brief speeches of welcome were made by the President and by Mr. John Brougham the First Vice-President of the Club. Mr. Toole responded in a witty and graceful address, after which there were speeches by Joseph Jefferson, William Stuart, A. Oakey Hall, John T. Ford, Isaac H. Bromley, and others.

In the course of the entertainment, a humorous and brilliant speech was made by Mr. William Winter, which he concluded by reading the following poem :—

JOHN LAURENCE TOOLE—A WELCOME.

(Lotos Club, August 6th, 1874.)

I.

The odour that all sense delights
Enchants us most on summer nights ;
And music, Nature's kindest boon,
Breathes gentlest underneath the moon :
For summer night and moonlight give
Quiet and grace in which we *live ;*
In which alone the inner soul
Finds, if not words, at least control,
And, for a moment, lifts us far
Towards realms where saints and angels are.
So Friendship's soft and tender voice
Sounds clearest when our hearts rejoice ;
For, when true gladness thrills the heart,
Selfish and sordid cares depart,
Dulness retires—and in their place
Comes the rich glow of peace and grace.
And then we see each other clear ;
The voice within the voice we hear ;

And deep thoughts surge to eye and cheek,
Nor words, nor smiles, nor tears can speak !
The old love-ditties that were sung,
The whispered vows, when we were young,
The silken touch of fragrant tress,
The maiden's awful loveliness,
Starlight and sea-breeze, beach and spray,
The sunshine of some sacred day,
A mother's kiss on lip and brow,
The tones of loved ones, silent now,
The light that never more will gleam,
The broken hope—the vanished dream—
All these come thronging through the brain,
Till, half with joy and half with pain,
Our souls break loose from common things
And soar aloft on angel wings,
Out of the tumult and the glare,
The fretful strife, the feverish care,—
To that great life of peace and grace
Which waits this suffering human race ;
That larger life than sight or sound,
Wherewith God's goodness folds us round.
This is the magic, this the power
That thrills, and crowns the festal hour.

II.

The summer, and the moon is bright,
And perfect gladness rules this night ;
And through our rapture, gracious, free,
A silver voice across the sea
In tender accents whispers sweet :
" Be kind to him whom now you greet !
By England's fireside altar-stone
His name is prized, his virtue known :
To England's heart his fame is dear ;
To him she gives her smile, her tear ;

She loves him for his rosy mirth ;
She loves him for his manly worth :
She knows him bright as morning dew :
She knows him faithful, tender, true ;
Her hope comes with him o'er the deep, —
With him to smile, with him to weep ;
Ah, give him friendship that endures,
And take him from her heart to yours !"—
That voice is heard !   By deed and cheer
We give him loyal welcome here !
In art's fair garden, where we stand,
We take him by the strong right hand ;
In friendship's cup the pledge we drain,
And bind him fast with friendship's chain !
Honour the man, whate'er his stage,
Who wields the arts to cheer the age !

III.

And oh, my friends, if I might say
(To point and close this humble lay)
What other voices float to me,
Across another, darker sea,
What words of cheer are wafted through
My fancy's realm, to him and you ;
Some music, then, indeed, might flow
Should make your hearts and pulses glow !
For then would ring out, rich and deep,
The royal tones of some who sleep—
The brilliant and the wise, too soon
Snatched from our side in manhood's noon :
Ere genius half her vigil kept ;
For whom our hearts and Morning wept ;
And these a welcome without stint—
My feeble words can only hint--

Would give this friend and comrade, come
So far from kindred and from home.
But, this denied, I prattle on—
The echo, when the music's gone—
With yet the hope that words well-meant
May find a grace, for good intent,
With you, companions tried and dear ;
With him the guest that's honoured here.
Nor will I think he views with scorn
These rhymes of welcome, lowly born ;
These wild-wood roses, faint but sweet,—
By kindness scattered at his feet.

V.

THE welcome accorded to the English comedian at Wallack's Theatre was of the most enthusiastic character. " His first words," says one of the leading critics, " ' There's always somebody on this stairway,' betrayed his identity before he appeared behind the footlights ; and when, as ' Hammond Coote,' he tripped briskly upon the stage, with his genial face scarcely disguised by his make-up as a middle-aged barrister of a good-natured, half-helpless, and wholly-lovable disposition, the thronged house rose at him, and for the space of two minutes. the clapping of hands, the rapping of canes, and the shouts of ' Toole ! Welcome !' and ' Toole again !' completely drowned the words which were uttered but not expressed. . . . When the curtain fell upon the first act of

Wig and Gown, there was not a doubtful mind in the audience, and the drop-curtain had hardly separated Mr. Toole from his critics before a storm of cheers summoned him to the front to receive as cordial a greeting as was ever vouch-safed to an actor in his trying but enviable situation."

Many floral tributes were handed over the foot-lights at the close of *The Spitalfields Weaver*, which finished the programme, and amongst them was a floral ship, presented by the passengers on the *Republic* who accompanied Mr. Toole across the Atlantic. It was quite a remarkable work of art, and was afterwards exhibited in the lobby of the theatre.

A week later Mr. Toole paid a visit to Long Branch, where a representative of the *New York Evening Mail* interviewed him, the writer stating in his introduction, that " few are gifted with so felicitous a manner as that possessed by Mr. Toole. Cordial, but acute, he receives visitors as friends, and makes them at home ; and, although speaking and acting with many English mannerisms, he is singularly free from those prejudices which have made some of his countrymen so unpopular in this country." Referring to his acting, the writer says : " His power of exciting to tears or laughter is unequalled ; but, admirable and amusing as are

his broad comedy parts, I coincide with the opinion
of many competent authorities in preferring his
rendering of serio-comic characters in which our
nobler passions are interested."

The interview, question and answer, is worth
repeating.

Q. What are your general impressions as to
America ?

A. I have been greatly surprised and delighted,
and shall be more so in a month's time if America
likes me as well as I like it.

Q. On your arrival at New York what astonished
you most ?

A. Blocks of buildings and blocks of ice.

Q. Which do you prefer ?

A. I have tasted a good deal of the latter, and
approve of it greatly when taken with straws and
sugar.

Q. Talking of drinks, how do you find the feed-
ing ?

A. First-rate. Some of the hotels give you
enough at one meal to last you for a week, and
the variety of vegetables particularly astonished
me. Who christened some of the dishes ? I
thought that clam chowder, gumbo and squash,
were relations of my attendant darkey, and that
he was imposing on my innocence, but now I have
made their acquaintance I find them much better

than " Le Roi Carotte " and all that sort of thing you know.

Q. Was your reception satisfactory ?

A. More than I could possibly have expected I have received the greatest kindness from all sorts of people. Through the kindness of friends, I have received the freedom of the Manhattan, Union, and Lotos Clubs, and the banquet given to me by the members of the last was intensely gratifying. Old friends and new faces welcomed me, and I rejoiced that I had left Old England to visit Greater Britain. Among those who have specially extended courtesies to me are Joe Jefferson, John Owens, Sothern, John Brougham, Mark Twain, Dan Bixby, Lawrence Barrett, Manager Stuart, Oakey Hall, Mr. H. Marston, Messrs. Jarrett and Palmer, J. Rutty, W. Floyd, J. L. Wallack, Theodore Moss, and the members of the Lotos Club.

Q. Have you seen much of the country ?

A. I have visited Niagara and Saratoga.

Q. What do you think of Niagara ?

A. The greatest sight I ever saw. I saw it the evening I arrived, and got up before daylight to see it again in case none of the water should be left. It can't last long anyhow, and I wrote to several of my London friends to come over soon, as I didn't believe it could go on at the same rate.

I told the hotel proprietor that I never knew any performance had such a "long run," but he assured me that he had made special arrangements that the fall season would continue till further notice. When we were under the falls I had to pay for my costume. This was the first time I had ever paid for "dressing up," as I generally receive pretty large sums for putting on eccentric costumes.

Q. What do you think of Saratoga ?

A. The vastness of the hotels surprised me. Also I felt a kindred feeling for the darkey hall-men. They sat along in a row like negro minstrels, and I was much astonished at the absence of bones and tambourine ; wondered whether the conundrums would be good, and finally asked the clerk which was Dan Briant, and when the show would commence.

Q. Did you taste the waters ?

A. I went through a course conscientiously, and they did not make me quite so unwell as our English mineral waters. Something out of a black bottle taken afterwards improves the taste, you know.

Q. What do you think of Long Branch ?

A. I think it is a very jolly place. Hotels remarkably good and bathing admirable, you know.

Q. What specially attracted your attention ?

A. My own portraits, which are spread all over the place, and I think make me look very serious. You will please inform the public that I do not intend to play *Richard III.* or *Othello;* my agent, Mr. Loveday, must slyly have told the photographer to give me a romantic appearance. I have heard a good many unconscious inquiries as to " that fellow Toole "—of course, I have my own opinion as to that, but modesty prevents my divulging it, you know.

Q. What do you think of the New York theatres ?

A. I have not seen Wallack's lighted yet, but consider it one of the best comedy theatres I ever entered.   All the arrangements seem very perfect. Very few of the rest are open, but I have visited Niblo's and Booth's, and was greatly impressed by their suitableness for spectacle and the splendour of decoration.

Q. What do you think of the ladies ?

A. Very charming.   The more I see of them the more I shall like them—particularly in the auditorium at Wallack's.

Q. What do you think of the Third Term ?

A. It is not fair to puzzle an unoffending stranger with conundrums.   I give it up.

Q. How do you like being interviewed ?

A. The process of extracting ideas is preferable to that of extracting teeth, particularly when the operator is so—you know what I mean, you know, and if you know—

Here Mr. Toole extracted a specimen of our fractional currency and began folding it up with great care. I pointed sternly to the final paragraph of the editorial advice to persons about to be interviewed and asked,—

Q. Can I oblige you with change on a 'bus ticket ?

A. Well, no, you know, not at present, very much obliged, you know.   Let's go to lunch.

The interview then closed.

HESPERUS.

P.S.—And very important.

CERTIFICATE OF VERACITY.

The above interview is real.   None others are genuine unless signed,

J. L. TOOLE.

VI.

THE *Tribune,* in its notice of 'Uncle Dick,' said :— " The test that Mr. Toole meets is this, that in conditions of circumstance which arouse the best emotions of average humanity his art makes him the perfect reflection of the nature of mankind.

The colour is English, but the fact is universal. . . . Mr. Toole makes no points, but conducts himself, whether in joy or in affliction, precisely as a humble, simple-minded, tender-hearted man might do in the circumstances suggested. There is a Peggotty-like scene for 'Uncle Dick' towards the close of the play, and in this Mr. Toole was surpassingly powerful—by dint of absolutely quiet intensity of suffering, threaded by jets of that humour which might flow out of the effort of a sweet nature to be kind and jolly under painful circumstances. To see this is to think in what a grand and splendid way affliction elevates even the commonest human being. Not moonlight on the ocean, nor sunset in the forest, can be more weirdly melancholy, more awful, or more sublime than the lofty state of anguish, striving to be cheerful, of a good man broken-hearted through his self-devoting affection."

The *Times* said, " Mr. Toole personates the noble, well-meaning hero of *Uncle Dick's Darling* with such fidelity to nature that we are puzzled how to criticize his acting."

The result of the Philadelphian criticisms may be summed up in the expressed hope that he would come back again. " He is an actor for whom one's liking increases with each time that he is seen."

Baltimore congratulated Mr. Ford, the manager of the Grand Opera House, on his engagement of an actor worthy of the brilliant audiences that assembled to greet him, the *Press* declaring that "his 'Artful Dodger' is the drollest and most enjoyable piece of acting we have seen for a long time. All other attempts at its presentation are complete failures compared with Mr. Toole's great success."

Cincinnati found in his 'Harry Coke,' in *Off the Line*, "unsurpassable tenderness and pathetic force."

Syracuse and Pittsburg were equally delighted with all his performances; and at critical Chicago we find one of the leading papers in the West, the *Inter-Ocean*, referring to *Dearer than Life* as "one of the best works of modern drama," and the representation of "Michael Garner" as "one of the most finished pieces of modern acting." "In view of the discussion now going on among the clergy and extremists of all denominations regarding the theatre," says the *Inter-Ocean*, "it is a question whether a better sermon has ever been preached, or a truer method inculcated, than that contained in the sterling honour, characteristic humour, delicate tenderness, and heroic self-sacrifice displayed by the plain but honest 'Michael Garner.' We can readily understand why Mr.

Toole has gained so high a reputation among his countrymen ; and, while a certain familiarity with London life is indispensable to a full appreciation of his inimitable truth to life, there is the broad element of human nature, and the deep sympathy with human feeling, which appeal to all alike wherever found. The character of 'Michael Garner' is one peculiar to London. It is the type of the sterling, honest shopkeeper—the man whose pride is his unblemished name and upright character. He may be vulgar, and, to the fastidious eyes of his would-be-genteel neighbours, he is vulgar, and yet in his heart of hearts he carries the delicacy and honour of a gentleman, and in his dealings with his fellows he never forgets his old friends, his early life, his parents, and his God. Such a man is ' Michael Garner,' and there is no actor now living who could more faithfully and more truly have stood in that Briton's shoes than Mr. Toole. His every action, his every attitude are perfect. The very manner in which he lifts his coat-tails, the way in which he expresses his joy, his welcome to his guests, his dress, his joviality, his anger, his pathos, all are true to life— truer than anything the stage has given us for many years. In this character Mr. Toole is more than a comedian ; he is great. We question whether Garrick himself ever exhibited a more finished piece of pantomime than where the old man trifles with his bread and thinks of those he loves."

St. Louis, Louisville, and in fact all the other cities that Mr. Toole visited, appear through their press to have been as thoroughly entertained and delighted as was the critic of the *Chicago Inter-Ocean*, and *Wig and Gown* being out of the bill, the whole of Mr. Toole's *répertoire* is cordially endorsed, and his company, more particularly Mr. Herbert, Miss Johnstone, and Mr. Westland, receive special marks of favour at the hands of the critics. The *Louisville Courier* regarded the "Dodger" as "a bit of character-sketching which, for artistic make-up and rendering, is not surpassed upon the stage the world over. We know of no actor who is more painstaking : he overlooks no detail, and there is originality in whatever he presents."

The *Cincinnati Gazette* was impressed with the remarkable individuality of each of Mr. Toole's characters, coupled with which "thoroughness in art" the writer found "a remarkable fidelity to nature, a fine sense of humour, and an artistic propriety which never steps outside the business of the play."

The Canadian papers were entirely unanimous in their praise of Mr. Toole's work, regarding him

as "a genial and masterly exponent of the richest
humour, and having an equal command of tender
pathos." The *Toronto Mail* and *Leader* vied with
each other in saying the pleasantest and most
complimentary things, as indeed did the leading
journals of the other cities. At Ottawa the first
night was spoken of in the journals as "a gala
night," and the last night was equally crowded and
festive. At Montreal the same; and the Dominion
parted with him with cordial expressions of regard.

VII.

"You had a curious experience at a certain
American city which was to be nameless," I said,
"the genial citizen who *would* take you home, and
when he got there was another man; do you
remember it? You told me the story years ago."

My host looks up at me for a moment with a
puzzled face, which presently beams with a genial
laugh.

"Oh! yes, I remember," he says; "it was at
——. Don't mention the place; he might not
like it, and I should be sorry to hurt his feelings.
Besides, he was the editor of the leading newspaper in the district, and had a rival journalist, of
course, and if that rival journalist got hold of the
story wouldn't his rival worry him! But you

know best about that. I am not a journalist. Actors have no rivalries, of course. I remember that American editor. 'You must stay with me, my dear Mr. Toole; you *must;* we will take no denial,' he said. He seemed a jolly, nice sort of fellow, and was so tremendously pressing that I gave way and went home with him; it was some distance, in the suburbs.

"At home he was a different man entirely. The wife was 'the boss.' She was a learned woman also: had quite a knowledge of literature and poetry. She fired off questions at me with regard to Thackeray and Dickens, and other celebrities. There were several children, they all stood round me and questioned me, cross-examined me.

"After a time they gave me a cup of tea. This was in the afternoon, instead of lunch or dinner.

"I went to the theatre, acted, and went home with him at night.

"After a little more questioning from his wife without any signs of refreshment, she asked me if, before I went to bed, I would have a cup of tea or a glass of water. Whereupon he, in a very humble way, said, 'We never take alcohol in this house.'

"I was so depressed and overweighted with the whole thing that I hadn't the courage to say I should like something to eat. I had a glass of water and went to bed.

" I couldn't sleep, however. I was frightfully hungry and tired; really thought of getting out of the window and running away, and should have done so if it had not been too high, although the city was at some distance. We had to drive to the house, which was in the suburbs.

" On saying ' good-night,' the wife informed me that they breakfasted at half-past seven, at which time it was clear I was expected to be up. So just as I was thoroughly exhausted, and could have slept a little, I was aroused, and had to turn out.

" I had breakfast, and then hoped to join Loveday at his hotel and get a little rest. But the wife said, ' Now, So-and-so, take Mr. Toole out and show him all the public buildings of ——.'

" And he did take me out, and began to show me all the public buildings. And once or twice I tried to slip away from him, in private rooms and corners, and get a wink of sleep. But he was the most persistent host I ever had.

" At last, in the midst of our tour of the public buildings, I gave him the slip, and fairly ran away; went to the hotel without my luggage, and nothing would induce me to leave it. I apologized to my host, I hope in as friendly a way as possible; but the very thought of the adventure even at this distance of time makes me shudder."

VIII.

" And now," said my genial host, " we are entitled to our holiday."

" A holiday for me, but work for you," I said.

" I long to get to work again," he replied ; " it seems years since I left off.   I felt as if I had been to Aix half my life until we began the other day to put the incidents of the time into your note-book. To-day is Wednesday.   I open at Whitby on Monday.   From there I go to Harrogate, beginning my tour quietly and in very pleasant places. Suppose we start for York on Friday, spend Saturday or Sunday there, go to the Cathedral, moon about, have a chat after dinner, and leave for Whitby Monday morning ?"

" Agreed," I said ; " and *au revoir*."

III.

OUR TRIP TO THE NORTH.

At York—Buying up the Press—A lesson in moral ethics—
The Cathedral and the Theatre—At the Yorkshire Blind
Asylum—Queer characters—A reminiscence of Downing
Street—Toole and Rabelais—Troublesome callers and
correspondents—The outside world and actors—"Orders"
—"Who's to pay me for my time?"—John Ryder and
his mysterious patron—Was he a bishop out of work?
—A visit to St. Mary's—Toole's pleasant fooling—The
story of "A Wonderful Old Dame at York."

I.

It was on a Friday in September, 1886, that we
stepped into the Great Northern express at King's
Cross, and arrived at York in time for dinner. In
the evening we took a walk in the direction of the
theatre. We found several of the newsboys of the
city congregated in the locality of the playhouse,
which was redeemed from the term "profane"
by the fact that it was within the shadow of the
Cathedral. Toole, finding the boys had had a
poor sale for their papers (at least they so informed him) bought up their remaining stock,

and then commenced to question them concerning the theatre. The scene of the interview was the pit and gallery entrance, and the boys numbered four, the eldest a lad of about fifteen, a knowing-looking fellow, who had the instinct of a diplomatist, but did not meet with the success that is usually supposed to accompany judicious lying.

"You never go into such a wicked place as that?" said Toole, pointing a warning finger at the theatre.

"No, sir," said the diplomatist, who took upon himself to be spokesman for the rest.

"You know better?"

"Yes, sir, I do," replied the diplomatist with a long, serious face.

"Go to Sunday school?"

"Oh, yes, sir," replied the diplomatist, counting his pennies.

"That's right, it is a good thing to go to Sunday school; do you all go?"

"Not me," said the smallest of the four, a bright-eyed, merry-looking little fellow.

"Why not?"

"My clothes ain't good enough."

"But you have been to the theatre, I can see you have; now don't deny it if it is true."

"Yes, I have, sir," said Bright-eyes, whose clothes were not good enough for Sunday school.

"Oh dear, oh dear!" Toole exclaimed, turning his head away in evident pain, and then once more facing the diplomatist: "but *you* wouldn't go to the theatre, whether your clothes were good enough or not?"

MR. TOOLE AND THE YORK NEWSBOYS.

"No, sir, I know how wicked it is."

"The devil's house, eh?"

"Yes, sir," said the diplomatist.

"Have *you* ever been inside the theatre?" Toole asked, addressing another of the four.

"Yes, sir, to pantomime."

"To pantomime!" Toole exclaimed, in a tone of encouragement.

"Yes, sir."

"Wasn't it fine?"

"It was, sir."

"Did you like the clown?"

"I did, sir!"

"So did I, when I was a boy! Would you like to go and see the play now?" the former severity of his manner having disappeared.

"I should, sir."

"And you?" asked Toole, addressing Bright-eyes.

"Yes, sir," was the prompt response.

"And *you?*" asked Toole, feeling in his pocket whence the coppers had come that had purchased the newspapers.

The face of the diplomatist was a study. His mouth twitched, his eyes wandered.

"You'll go home if your wicked companions go into the devil's house, eh?" said Toole.

"I don't know, sir," said the diplomatist, almost tearfully.

"Now you *have* been in there" (pointing to the gaily-lighted entrance to the pit, decorated with bills of the play depicting the fun of an American company), "that's why you are troubled?"

" Yes, sir, only to pantomime."

" There; don't tell any more stories about it," said Toole, " never tell stories, let this be a warning to you; it is not wicked to go and be amused at a theatre, if you are good boys, do your work, and are honest, and go to church or chapel. There, come along."

The four youngsters followed the comic teacher into the entrance-hall of the palace of delight, he paid for their admission, and we followed to get a peep at them from the pit. The house was not crowded; they found room in the front-row seats of the gallery. The diplomatist was the first to make his appearance and to take what he considered to be the best seat; presently they were all roaring with laughter at some of the practical American fun, Bright-eyes clapping his hands when the scene was over, with intense enjoyment. " They are happy," said Toole, as we left the pit, " we have bought up the Press and bribed the publishers; now let us go and see what is going on in front of the house."

II.

THE main entrance to the Theatre at York is quite a good example of ecclesiastical architecture, as if the Cathedral authorities had said to themselves, "We cannot avoid having this profane house here, but we will try and disguise it;" and they have done so most effectually. If they made a persistent effort to see that the entertainments given within were in accordance with the high spirit they suggest in the portico, it would be better for art, and none the worse for the growing diplomatists and the children who cannot go to Sunday school because their clothes are not good enough. I don't know that the York ecclesiastics do not patronize the theatre, but I have had some experience of Cathedral cities, and I have not known one of them where the followers of the profession of Shakspere, Ben Jonson, Garrick, Kean, Macready, and the rest were not as a rule regarded askance and left to perform if not to empty benches at least to a house free from the patronage of the Church. The religious people of provincial cities forget that the theatre must always degenerate where the light and leading of a district neglect it, and thus fail to secure, if not the highest and artistic performances, at least such as shall not pander to the brutalized passions of those whom education does not redeem from the worst vices.

The entertainment was more than half over. The front of the house was in semi-darkness. A solemn porter sat within the gloomy portals. We affected to regard the place as a church or meeting-house. He was a stolid Yorkshireman. He was not going to bother himself about a couple of fools who didn't know a theatre from a chapel. Presently Toole, addressing him in a serious voice, not above a whisper, asked if it would be possible to hire the place.

" Hoire it ?" he replied. " I dussay."

" We might like to give a missionary service here," said Toole, with a touch of the Mawworm grimace.

" Indeed !" said the porter.

" In aid of the Chocktaw Indians," Toole went on, "a much neglected race."

" Aw' can give you no information, yo'll ev to see t' manager."

" Indeed," said Toole, " I suppose there is a service now going on."

" Aye," said the porter, as if it was not worth his while to call the play anything else.

" Might we look in ?" said Toole.

" You mought," replied the porter.

Toole took off his hat and we entered, the porter watching us as we went up to the office and took our tickets in presence of two character portraits of Toole, one as the " Dodger," the other as " Paul Pry." Presently it was whispered all over the place that Toole was in the house; then there was a good deal of " How-do-you-do, Mr. Toole! Very good of you to come in and see us," and so on ; and then we saw that the porter had joined the little complimentary crowd, and though he continually fell into silent fits of internal mirth, he made no noise, but doubled himself up and had private and noise-less struggles with himself against what is called bursting with laughter.

III.

THE next morning we strolled about York, "hung upon the bridge," and questioned the right of the toll-man to charge us for crossing ; then tried to arrange with him a payment down to cover the time we should remain, as we might find it neces-sary to cross the bridge very often ; finally offered to buy the bridge and release the citizens from the tax, and so on, all in a pleasantly serious way, and to the advantage of the toll-keepers in the end, whether they would or no ; for Toole objects to study character, as he calls it, for his own amusement and instruction, without the offer of a solatium for any trouble or chagrin on the part of the character studied.

Later in the day we called upon Mr. Buckle, the accomplished master of the Yorkshire School for the Blind. Two years previously Toole had given a performance to the children, boys and girls. When we entered the schools, after a stroll in the grounds, Mr. Buckle said, " Don't speak, I would like to see if they remember you."

We went into the girls' school first. The pupils all rose as we entered. Some of them were verging upon young-womanhood.

" I have brought a friend to see you," said the master.

They smiled, some of them turning their sightless eyes towards the master with an expression of inquiry upon their calm faces.

At a sign Toole spoke.

" Good morning, young ladies," he said.

" Who is it ? " asked the master.

One of the girls, hesitating hardly a moment, and with a pleased and confident manner, exclaimed, " Mr. Toole ! " which was followed by a general exclamation of " Mr. Toole ! "

" I am very glad you remember me again," said Toole, "and I hope you are all well ; you look well."

" Yes, thank you, Mr. Toole," said several voices.

In the boys' department the same test was applied. The boys did not respond, however, at once. They appeared more anxious than the girls.

"Don't you remember *Trying a Magistrate?*" asked Toole.

"Yes, yes." said two voices at once; it is Mr. Toole," and the whole school laughed spontaneously.

The comedian chatted with the boys for a little time, telling them he had heard they had given a public concert, and how pleased he was to learn that it had been a great success.

The Yorkshire School for the Blind has the reputation among experts of being the best and most practical of its kind in existence. It is less of a show school than some, but it is very thorough in its work, the headmaster possessing all the knowledge and patience necessary to make good teachers and happy pupils. Mr. Buckle is a University man, and is, among other accomplishments, an artist-etcher of considerable skill and taste. "The Historie of the King's Manor House" at York, by R. Davies, F.S.A., is exquisitely illustrated by Mr. Buckle, the work being not only a labour of love from an artist's point of view, but for the reason that the King's Manor House at York is the home of the Blind School, which shares the grand old place with the National School for Boys; and within the precincts of the beautiful remains of St. Mary's Abbey, which contains the King's Manor House, are the Museums of Natural History and Antiquities, belonging to the Yorkshire Philosophical Society. The ruins of St. Mary's Abbey are singularly picturesque, and Mr. Buckle's pupils seem to have full licence to ramble through the lovely turf-like grounds that surround them. We spent some time on Sunday with Mr. Buckle and his family. His pupils and their monitors seemed to be quite a part of his household. They all appeared to be very happy, both boys and girls, and had many sources of amusement. At the Cathedral, which we attended, they were earnestly devout, but took more interest in the singing than in any other part of the service. They remained to hear the voluntary, and enjoyed it immensely ; one of the boys is himself a fine organist, and several are excellent musicians. When they returned from the service to go home, the boys, in companies of six or eight, touched each other's shoulders with their hands and, keeping thus together, walked away without any difficulty, and as we strolled along among the good York folk who had been to church, Mr. Buckle told us many interesting stories of the wonderful things the blind can do both in the industrial and fine arts. All this entertained us immensely, and I felt a special interest in Mr. Buckle's revelations, having myself, in association with the Bishop of Worcester, the Rev. Mr. Blair, Dr. Williams, and a select committee, projected and assisted to found the Worcester School for the Blind, our chief object being the popularization of the Roman alphabet, the first embossed example of the local printing of which I executed upon my own press in the ancient city of " the crowning mercy." But enough of myself. The next morning a bulky package went to the schools ; it contained many examples of chocolates, purchased that morning in York, and the authority of Mr. Buckle was besought for a distribution of the same " with Mr. Toole's love " on the earliest fitting occasion.

IV.

" Among the queer characters I have met, I recall," he said, " a very egotistical fellow who never talked about anybody but himself : not that he had anything interesting to say about himself, but he talked of nothing but how he lived ; what time he got up, how he breakfasted, when he lunched, what he ate, when he went to bed, and how he was in a general way. I have often thought of him as a suggestion for character. A sort of man who when he gets up in the morning says, ' How am I, to-day ?' and who carries that spirit of selfishness, unconscious or otherwise, throughout his life. It is never with him, 'How are you, to-day?' but

MR. TOOLE AS "CHAWLES."

'How am I? Let me look at my tongue. How is my pulse? *How am I?*'"

The point of the following reminiscence is also one example of this genuine sense of humour, which it has just occurred to me to mention, though I hope these volumes teem with similar illustrations.

"I have several times had the pleasure of breakfasting with Mr. Gladstone. He wrote a letter to me after he saw 'Chawles' and *Ici* at the Globe : wrote and asked if I would go and lunch or breakfast with him. I went, and he was very complimentary, expressed great pleasure at my performances. We talked about theatres. In regard to the influence of audiences upon actors, he related to me a story about Young in Edinburgh. Young was playing 'Iago.' In the first act he was not at all up to the mark. At the end of the second an intimate friend went round and said, 'Why, Young, you played this second act far better than the first—a different thing altogether!' 'Yes,' Young replied, 'Scott came into a box at the beginning of the second act.' 'Yes,' I said in reply, 'one does, as it were, get inspiration from a special audience sometimes, not that I would wish to disparage the general and regular audiences ; but from the moment you came into the theatre, the night before last, to see *Ici on Parle Français*, I felt that I played 'Spriggins' with a new zest.

"On the second occasion when I breakfasted with Mr. Gladstone, Lord Tennyson was there, and two or three clergymen. I was deeply impressed both with the statesman and the poet ; very much surprised at Mr. Gladstone's conversational powers. He talked to me about theatres and dramatic art ; then to Tennyson about other things, and to the clergymen about Church affairs; then about science to a savant. He told me several theatrical anecdotes, and seemed to talk just as well on every subject. That was at Harley Street. I afterwards breakfasted with him in Downing Street ; Professor Blackie was there. The conversation rose to such a high and elevated platform that, when I left and found myself in the street, I talked to a policeman to try and bring myself down to the level of ordinary life."

v.

I HAVE said that Toole has a quaint sense of humour ; and over supper, at York, I had several striking illustrations of it. Humour is of no period nor nationality. We were talking of memory, and how it is cultivated to a marvellous power by actors.

" Has it ever struck you," he asked, " what possible quackery there is in this new business of memory teaching ?" and he went on to answer his own question as clever story-tellers and modern ballad-makers do. " I often think of a capital illustration of the nonsense of these memory men when I see their advertisements. A man pays two guineas and takes lessons. At the end of his course he returns, rings the bell—' What is it ?' they ask. 'I have forgotten my umbrella ! '"

This is akin to Rabelais' satire of Panurge consulting Herr Trippa the astrologist, who could forecast and tell all things to come, and was intended to typify a famous German sage ; and who foretold Panurge how he should be deceived and disgraced by his wife when he married ; and who, knowing everything, did not know that while he was prating to the king or Panurge, the pages and lacqueys about the Court were making love successfully to his wife, who was passable fair and a pretty snug hussy ; that, indeed, what he was so solemnly predicting for another was happening to himself.

VI.

" I sometimes think you might make a chapter out of the curious men I have met, and another about theatrical ' orders,' " said my friend and host.

" Don't you think we have already described a few of your discoveries in this direction ? "

" Yes, of course. ' How am I ?' is a good one ;

might be worked up, eh ? Would make a capital character in a play. The loafers who call on one to beg and borrow are full of character ; I don't allude to the genuine cases of distress, but to the men who make a business of it.

" I remember a fellow meeting me in Dublin some years ago, rushing up to me, with great volubility, ' Ah, my dear Toole, my dear John Toole, I am so glad to see ye looking so well,' taking my hand in both his and grasping it most cordially. ' Can I have ten minutes with ye—just ten minutes ? I have a matter of importance to talk to ye about.'

" I saw at once that he was a borrower, and a flashy one ; not a man you could put off with a sovereign. So I told him I was very busy just then, and was very much bothered, had been losing money lately, and should very much like to have ten minutes with him ; and asked if he thought he could lend me 300*l.*

" ' Good Lord, no ! Me lend you 300*l.* ! '

" Well, I said, perhaps some of his friends might. However, if he would come round to me that evening after the play, or meet me at the hotel, I would like to talk it over with him.

" Oh, very well, of course he would come. Of course I never saw him afterwards."

" And have you not met some odd and eccentric

ladies, as well as odd and eccentric men in your time ? " I asked.

" Yes," he replied, " I have, and they are among the most troublesome of my correspondents ; more troublesome than men because one can't be rude to them.   For instance, the dear old ladies who never go to theatres, and yet beg one to ' Try a Magistrate ' at their bazaars, or sing ' The Speaker's Eye ' at their tea-parties.   Don't you think one has reason to be annoyed when Lady Fitzboodle, at one of these social functions, as it is the fashion to call tea-parties now-a-days, says, ' Oh, thank you so much, Mr. Toole, it is so kind of you ; I never go to a theatre, therefore it is doubly kind of you to favour us in this way ; ' I need not say I have declined to favour that identical ladyship again ; I suppose it is thoughtlessness this kind of thing."

" Call it eccentricity," I said.

" Well, I don't mind ; there must be all kinds of people to make up the great world, but there are some kinds one could do without.

" There is a dear old lady in Glasgow who only reads two books, Shakspere and the Bible ; and has never read, she tells me, any other.   I always call and talk to her. She has seen Edmund Kean and Liston, and all the great actors, and is still as fond of the play as ever ; fresh, bright, and interesting ;

quotes frequently from her two books, the Bible and Shakspere. A very cheerful, bright playgoer, very different from the lady whom I mentioned

MR. TOOLE IN "THE STEEPLECHASE."

in my speech at the Rosebery banquet, who thought I must be a gay man because I went to the theatre every evening.

" How strangely little the outside world knows of actors and acting after all; and how firmly rooted is the prejudice against both!   There is another old lady, who is, in fact, a relative of mine, who had been brought up not to go to theatres ; but after many years she made up her mind to see me act.   But in order to see me under what she considered far more proper conditions than those which applied to a theatre, she went to see me at the Crystal Palace.   She was very much entertained, and wanted to see me in another piece, and she then came a step nearer to the region of impropriety ; she came to the theatre at a morning performance, thinking that that was less wicked than going in the evening.

" And mind you, there is a lot of this nonsense going on, this compounding with sin, as it were, this bargaining with conscience ; there are many worthy people who try and persuade themselves that it is not in the least wrong to see *The Steeple-chase* at the Crystal Palace, but who would feel quite wicked if they came to see the same play at a London theatre.   In the same way thousands go to German Reed's and see every kind of dramatic entertainments, comedies, operas, farces, who would never dream of going to a theatre.   I am not blaming them ; it is their affair, not mine, and they get their money's worth at German Reed's, but it is very funny how people can be so illogical ; and, after all, the theatre began in the Church ; the clergymen were among the first actors, and some of their religious plays, I believe, were of a very remarkable and sensational character.

"But we were talking of 'orders'; that is another curious subject. Some people who can well afford to pay will do any mean kind of thing to get an order for the theatre. I have known ladies and gentlemen drive gaily up to King William Street in their carriages and pair, attended by powdered footmen, and present with pride an order for a box, or a couple of unnumbered tickets for the stalls. There are men who seem to think it is a kind of endorsement of position to be able to get an order to go into a theatre. I remember, when I was a very young actor, a friend saying he hoped I should take a theatre because it would be so jolly to know where he could always get orders. I receive curious letters for orders, with curious reasons why I should send them. A chemist's assistant wrote for an order, his claim being that he had once prepared a prescription for me, and had made up the wrong medicine, fortunately without injury ; and this had always made him follow my career with the greatest interest. Another applicant for dress-circles said he was emboldened to ask the favour because he had once met my uncle on board a steamer. Buckstone said when he became a manager he had to give up writing pieces, his time was so much occupied in writing orders. And yet Charles Mathews once told me of 'the boots' at a country hotel where he was staying asking to be paid for going to the theatre. Mathews, struck with the fellow's civility, gave him an order for the play.

"'Come and see the piece, Tom,' said Mathews.

"'At the theatre?'

"'Yes,' said Mathews. 'Here is an order for you.'

"The next day Mathews said, 'Well, Tom, did you like the play?'

"'Oh, yes,' said the boots, in a dubious kind of way; 'but who's to pay me for my time?'

"There are extremes, you see, in all things; the people who will carry on a perfect intrigue to get an order, and 'the boots' who wants to be paid for his time.

"Billington tells a good story, which I commend to the consideration of the order-fiend. A Yorkshire friend of Billington's came to London. Billington asked him if he was coming to the theatre.

" ' Of course,' he said ; ' I'm coming to see thee act.'

" ' When ? '

" ' To-morrow night.'

" ' Very well,' said Billington, ' I'll send you an order ; how many for—yourself and wife ? '

" ' I shall bring the missus,' said the Yorkshire-man, ' but I want no orders, lad ; how's thy mester to pay thee thy salary if thou lets folk in for nowt ? '

" That is a point the order-monger never seems to think of. A theatrical manager does not ask his butcher to give him an order for a sirloin, and he expects to pay his tailor and his grocer. When I was a lad in a wine-merchant's office, as I have before mentioned, I used, certainly, to get and to give wine-tasting orders for the docks—that was an old custom, you know, and may obtain to some extent now, but it pretty well ruined more than one firm. A bad thing, orders, bad for every-body—' for him that gives and him that receives,' as Shakspere says !

" There are certain persons whom one considers to be entitled to the privileges of the house ; but, as a rule, these persons are most considerate, and when business is exceptionally good they are quite sensitive about asking for seats ; they under-stand, of course, what an expensive thing the management of a theatre is, while many irresponsible and thoughtless order-hunters, if ever they do think about it, seem to imagine that the lessee of a theatre is only in fun, and that he opens his house simply for the pleasure of writing orders for all who have the audacity or the assumed friendliness to apply for them."

VII.

PRESENTLY our conversation turned upon travel and international affairs, notably in regard to French and English art.

"There have been several efforts on the part of English theatrical companies to capture Paris," said Toole. "I don't think any of them can be said to have succeeded. The only one of which I have any knowledge was what the Americans would call the Ryder and Swinburne combination. It was an excellent company, including Mr. Charles Wyndham, Mrs. Arthur Sterling, and others ; but is said not to have been brilliant in the way of management. How I came to know anything about it was in this way.

"It was during my engagement at the Gaiety. I had taken a holiday with my family and was returning home from Switzerland with George

Loveday and my son Frank. I saw an announcement of *Hamlet* at the Athénée,[1] a theatre which, by the way, was underground. On inquiry I heard that affairs were rather sixes and sevens,

[1] The Paris correspondent of the *Pall Mall Gazette* says :— " The English troupe which has come over here to perform Shakspere has chosen a very unpropitious moment. There is hardly any one in town, and the remaining inhabitants prefer the shores of the lakes of the Bois de Boulogne and Vincennes during this torrid weather to the theatre. It is true that *Hamlet* is being performed in a kind of cellar, where the *paradis* is below the level of the Seine, where one has to descend to the upper boxes, and that the Athénée is the coolest of playhouses. Still the weather is too hot. In addition to this, it is reckoned that only 20,000 Frenchmen in Paris understand English, and that 15,000 of these are engaged in commercial pursuits. It is remembered with shame how Macready could not draw an audience, and how, with tears in his eyes, he rushed from the stage, exclaiming that Paris would always be the capital of Bœotia. However, modern languages are now to be seriously studied, and we may live to see Shakspere appreciated in the original. The few critics who have ventured to the Athénée speak well of the performance, in spite of the difficulties surrounding it. A portion of the scenery belongs to *Une Folie à Rome*, and an Italian terrace serves for that at Elsinore. M. Auguste Vitu says that the actors, all Horse Guards, are much too large for the stage, and resemble a troupe of whales disporting themselves in an aquarium. He and Theodore Banville were the only two critics who were able to sit out the performance. He found Mr. Ryder, whom he terms ' *un grand diable* of an Englishman,' more like Don Quixote than the Prince of Denmark, and yet he admired his diction and his playing, and declared that he well deserved the applause with which the spectators greeted him. The parts of the Ghost, Laertes,

that there was no prospect of any great success ; not, as I have said before, on account of the artists, but owing to the want of proper direction, and also proper appreciation ; for after all, the French never did, and never will, believe that there are actors outside their own country, particularly English actors.

" I was passing a swell stationer's, and seeing an example of a very fine sheet of letter-paper, with a wonderful crest upon it, an idea occurred to me.   I went in, and after a time came out with that impressive piece of stationery. With the assistance of my travelling companions, I wrote a letter to Ryder, which, elegantly translated into French, I had beautifully transcribed upon that superb sheet of letter-paper, which was then duly folded up, sealed, and delivered by special messenger. The letter, which was inscribed with a name not unknown in the country of France, was something to the effect that the writer had observed with great pleasure that Mr. Ryder was

Polonius, and the Gravedigger were, in his opinion, very ably filled ; while Miss Cleveland and Miss Margaret Cooper played the Queen and Ophelia most satisfactorily, the latter lady being especially commendable for the talent, charm, and poesy which she threw over her *rôle*. M. Vitu thinks that many French actors would do well to go and see our countrymen struggling against the slings and arrows of outrageous fortune."—*Era*, August, 1873.

about to appear on the Paris stage as ' Hamlet,'
supported by a powerful English company. The
writer had seen Mr. Ryder in London, had
always greatly admired him as an interpreter of
Shakspere ; and it was also with satisfaction that
he noted among the company the name of Mr.

MR. JOHN RYDER.

Swinburne, whom he had also, in company with
his friend, Mr. Rothschild, seen upon more than
one occasion. He was quite sure that Paris would
welcome artists of their great and deserved
renown, and, so far as he could help their enter-
prise, he should commit himself to the adventure

with pride and pleasure.   Nothing tended more to
cement the friendship of the two great countries
than an interchange of artistic entertainments, and
he added, by the way, that he had just purchased

RYDER AND TOOLE IN PARIS—A LITTLE JEST.

a little château a few miles from Paris, where he
would be very pleased to welcome Mr. Ryder and
any of the leading members of his company—
indeed, so far as their professional engagements

would permit, he would be glad if they would make this château their home during their stay in Paris. Meanwhile, he desired them, if possible, to meet him that evening in the courtyard of the Grand Hotel at about half-past eleven. He would then communicate his views and suggestions to them, which he hoped would advance the prospects of their visit ; although, apart from any service he could render, he was quite sure they would meet with a great success.

"I only heard afterwards that on the night in question there was a special dress rehearsal for *Hamlet*, the close of which was considerably hastened in order that Mr. Ryder might keep an important engagement at the Grand Hotel. 'It's all right, ladies and gentlemen,' he said. ' Have no fear. We have had our little troubles and difficulties, but the thing will be a great go.' Whereupon he drew from his breast-pocket an important-looking letter, which he tapped in a knowing way, remarking, ' Here it is : here is the positive assurance ; Paris is going to take us up— English and French. You'll see, Swinburne, come with me : you must join me in this appointment.'

"However, this is by the way. I only heard it from a member of the company some time afterwards in London.

"At half-past eleven, Frank, myself, and Love-day sauntered from our rooms into the courtyard of the Grand Hotel. There, sitting together at one of the little round tables, were Ryder and Swinburne; Ryder evidently laying down the law to Swinburne, Swinburne receiving the law in his usual gloomy fashion. Swinburne was never a cheerful man—we used to call him 'Melancholy Tom;' but Ryder, as you know, was a noisy, genial, outspoken, overpowering kind of good fellow.

"All at once Ryder saw me, and starting up, exclaimed, 'Why, Johnnie, who'd have thought of seeing you here!'

"My natural response was, 'And who'd have thought of seeing you here!'

"'Me!' he exclaimed. 'Why, I appear on Monday as 'Hamlet.' I've got a company here, have been rehearsing several days—dress re-hearsal to-night, in fact.'

"Then we sat down and talked over his enter-prise. Loveday and Frank joined us, and I sug-gested a fear as to his success; said I didn't think the French would accept an English interpretation of Shakspere—expressed my great wonder that they condescended even to play Shakspere them-selves. But Ryder assured me that there was no doubt about the success of the present venture, anyhow—he had full assurance of it.

" Tom Swinburne looked at his watch, and muttered something about an appointment over-due. Ryder comforted him with the remark that these swells had so many engagements that they must be allowed a little grace.

" We continued to talk. Time slipped away. They grew very anxious.

" I invited them to supper. They said no, they must wait to keep an appointment. And then, I suppose by way of taking a friendly in-terest in my proceedings, Ryder said : 'And what may be your business in Paris ? '

" I began to feel a little sorry for the dis-appointment I had prepared for them ; and as I couldn't stay and give them a lift on the night of *Hamlet*, I began to show my hand.

" ' The fact is,' I said, ' I have been purchasing a little château a few miles outside Paris—'

" ' A what ? ' said Ryder.

" ' A château.'

" ' What do you mean—purchasing a little château ? '

" ' Well, that is exactly what I do mean. I have been buying a little château a few miles outside Paris, and I shall be pleased to welcome you and any of the leading members of your company—indeed, so far as your professional engagements will permit, I hope you will make this château your home during your stay in Paris.'

" ' Oh! you scoundrel ! ' exclaimed Ryder, producing the letter. ' Then, this is your work ! Oh, you ruffian ! you double-dyed villain ! ' adding in the same breath, ' Not a word of it outside this company, on your soul, Toole, until we are well out of Paris.'

" I gave him the pledge ; we had supper together, and I need not say we parted good friends. Ryder and Swinburne kept their own counsel with the company, maintaining to the last that success was assured ; but afterwards finding an explanation for the want of success in the fact that Paris had failed to appreciate the Ryder's subtle impersonation of the melancholy Dane."

VIII.

" I REMEMBER some years ago," said Toole, as we took an early walk the next morning, prior to leaving York for Whitby, where he was to play that night the opening engagement of his autumn tour, " attending the afternoon service at Chester. I never go to a cathedral city without finding my way to the afternoon service, and I hope I go in a thoroughly religious frame of mind, though I am more especially fond of the music, and think it most impressive, most soul-stirring. Lingering

to listen to the piece they play you out with—no,
I don't mean that, it is the voluntary—I noticed

"I THOUGHT HE MUST BE A BISHOP."

a very dignified gentleman pausing too. It was a
small congregation, and I could not help thinking

that even most of them had come to enjoy the
music. The tall, handsome old gentleman attracted my attention. He was dressed in black—
one of the long coats worn by the clergy; he
carried in one hand a pair of gold-rimmed glasses,
in the other a sober-looking book bound in dark,
rich cloth; I thought it might be a missal; he was
a remarkably dignified man, with white hair, a
shiny hat, had gaiters to his boots, and walked
very quietly; I thought he must be a bishop out
of work; no, I don't mean that, a bishop or a
dean, say, or some other great dignitary, in residence who is not acting—I mean preaching—but
who likes to go to the cathedral and set a good
example. When the organ ceased I walked
away; so did several others of the congregation,
and so likewise did the bishop—I felt sure he
was a bishop—and I was surprised to find him
evidently making gradually towards me. The
next moment he was by my side, and the next he
had smiled and passed me, remarking as he did
so, and in a very confidential kind of way, ' You'll
have a better audience than this to-night, Mr.
Toole.' "

IX.

WE had been advised to see St. Mary's Church

before we left York, and had arrived at the gates as Toole concluded his reminiscence of Chester. There are several St. Marys in York, and I do not recall which it was, the architectural and antiquarian interest of the place being rather eclipsed by one of those impromptu comedies on life's real stage which make a trip with Toole sometimes " as good as a play." We entered an old-fashioned kind of yard before reaching the church. There were what appeared to be almshouses on one side and the church on the other. It was very quiet, and, the morning being dull, rather gloomy. Several gravestones, which at some time or another had been removed in the course of local improvements, had been propped against the houses, and at last had settled into the earth as if the houses were mausoleums and the stones their records. We had to apply to an old lady living in one of the houses for the key of the church.

" Odd place for tombstones," said Toole.

" Varry," she said. " When they asphalted t'yard they moved t'stones and put 'em there, and forgot to put 'em back."

" Dear me," said Toole, turning a serious face to me, taking out a pocket-book and making a note. " This must be seen to. Meanwhile, we will look at the church."

" Varry well," she said, with an air of familiar

indifference, as much as to say, " You know best.
I've no objection.   Here's the key."

She was a very matter-of-fact person, no nonsense about her; fearless in the performance of
her duty, independent in her criticism of others, a
business-like, sturdy old dame.   She opened the
church doors ; she showed us an old font.   Toole
suggested that it was not in a good place for
examination.   She said he was " not t'first as had
said so."   He made several other remarks sugges-
tive of a rearrangement of various things, which
elicited an important fact, namely, that the vicar
of the parish had not been in the church for over
six months.   Toole whispered a " thought so "
to me, and our guide twirled her big key between
her finger and thumb, and in her keen way spotted
the fact that Toole was evidently a person in
official authority connected with the Church, an
Ecclesiastical Commissioner, or something of the
kind.   Thereupon she began to fence with his
questions, though she did admit that a vicar ought
not to leave his parish for six months at a time,
and she was willing to allow that there ought to
be no disputes nor misunderstandings in a Christian community.   At the same time she said it
was no business of hers what the vicar did or what
tenets he preached ; she did her duty, and her life
and that of her old man was known to their

neighbours; "as for what ye call Church disci-
pline, I donnat knaw what it is, and I donnat
wish to say anything agen nobody; w'en all gotten our fauts, and there let it rest!"

"But I *wish* you to speak your mind freely,"
said Toole, turning to me and remarking in a loud
whisper something to this effect (we were in the
porch now)—"Official duties—not always agreeable—honest old person teaches me—reprehen-
sible neglect—vicar must be seen to"—(then
quite privately, "Let us go out, don't like joking
in the church, though some people hereabout
evidently quarrel in it, which is much worse"),
and by this time the creaking lock once more
shut in the ancient font.

In the yard, the tombstones leaning against the
humble but somewhat picturesque dwellings were
referred to as evidence of a want of respect both
to the living and the dead.

"You would like them removed," said Toole.

"Well," she said, "it isna' pleasant having
gravestones at one's front door and leaaning again
one's hoose."

"No; I wish I had had your complaint before
me when the change was made."

"Well, we didna' loike to say much, you
see, because they said as it ud only be tem-
pory."

" Just so, just so," said Toole, with very much of the manner of the soap-boiler in *The Upper Crust*, "just so."

By this time one or two of the neighbours came to their doors, and the keeper of the key's old man.

" I'm not one as is fond of complaining," she said, now conscious of an audience before whom she would like to stand well, " but gravestones as companions isna' a thing as ye'd take to by choice."

" Certainly not," said Toole, " they shall be removed.   When will it be convenient for the cart to fetch them away ? "

" Oh, any time," said the dame, looking round at her audience for their approving nods, which came with much promptitude.

" Next week," said the comedian, making a fresh note in his book.   " And you are pretty comfortable in your homes ? " looking at the rest, though no one but the lady with the key ventured to speak ;   they evidently thought she was getting on so well, it would be a pity to interfere.

" Why, we mustna complain.   Some folks think we doonnat pay rent ; but we do ! "

" Indeed," said Toole, " it is so long since any of these matters have come before me that—I was under the impression that these were almshouses, that in fact they belonged to our Trust, so to speak."

" That may be," she replied, " but we has to pay rent, for all that ; it isna much, but when times is hard—"

" I see," said Toole, " you do not wish to pay rent."

" Yo've hit it," said the dame.

"You are not singular in that," said Toole, " there are quite a number of persons who do not wish to pay rent, and some who actually refuse to do so. We must see to your case ; but one thing at a time ; always a mistake to be in a hurry."

" Yes, sir, and thank you ; they do say in these parts, ' moast haste less speed,' but it isna often we'n pleasure of seein' one of t' Trustees feace to feace, and one as'll listen to what poor folks 'as gotten to say "—a remark which drew forth a murmur of applause from the bystanders.

" Just so," said Toole ; " well, I do not know what to say about the rent, but I will look into the matter ; as for these pieces of antiquity, the cart shall see to them at once."

" Shall my mester be digging 'em up ready ?"

" No," said Toole, " wait for the waggon—I mean the cart, and meanwhile, here is a little ' doosoar,' make what use you please of it, save it

up towards the rent, whitewash your places with
it, or turn it into a little extra tea," whereupon he
dropped a coin into the old dame's hand, and we
said "good day" to the wondering neighbours.

" Hope they will not be too much disappointed
about the cart—hope they won't wait too long for
the waggon, and we'll all take a ride.   But it is
too bad, isn't it, to go and dig up a churchyard,
asphalt the court, and leave the stones propped
up against the houses ?   Odd old lady, strong
face ; she wouldn't flinch, whatever her duty
might be.   Did you notice how she nursed that
key—reminded me of Durdles, somehow—and
did you notice that all the women wrapped their
arms up in their aprons ?   The old man hasn't
much to say about the rent or anything else, eh ?
—a wonderful old dame !"

IV.

CHATS BY THE WAY, AND JESTS.

" And Satan finds some mischief still for idle hands to do "—
The new, true, and impromptu comedy of " Tip it with
Green "—Sothern and the ironmonger—Mr. Lee and life
in New York—Florence and Sothern—Reminiscences of
Johnnie Clarke—Professional jealousies—" Dot" at New-
castle-on-Tyne—" Irving tells a capital story of Toole "—
A politic driver—"The Bell of the Abyss "—Travel in
England and America—George Loveday's opinion of
Toole.

I

At last it was time for our train to Whitby. We
were early. The train was late. We had bought
all the newspapers, and tipped all the porters.
Our carriage-door was locked. We were to have
no companions. Every moment we were expect-
ing the train to start, and every moment it did
nothing of the kind. " Satan finds some mischief still for idle hands to do." We made
several inquiries about the delay of the train ;
it was quite a remarkable delay ; it lasted
nearly half an hour. At last Toole, always bent
on amusing me or studying character, said we
must " do something." They were painting the

railway station (no reference is intended to a famous picture of a rival station in town), and doing the work with much elegance of design and detail. The company is proud of its station at York, as well it may be, and they had evidently resolved that the art spirit of the age should not be neglected in its decoration. The pillars supporting the magnificent roof were of a greyish tint of light blue, with a band of magenta at the base, and here and there at given points of the pillars themselves a similar band breaking into light filagree ornamentation. The armorial bearings of the company were emblazoned on pillars and columns, and altogether the work was of a very artistic character. A painter with a small brush, almost like a camel-hair pencil, was finishing the more delicate details of the most important of the decorations; he was earnestly engaged upon a piece of foliated work that ran round one of the pillars.

Toole called a boy, gave him some coppers, requested him to jog the painter's elbow and ask him—referring to the decorative scroll—"if he was going to tip it with green?"

We were too far away, of course, to hear anything, but we could see the painter offering some kind of explanation to the boy, the boy pointing to our carriage.

The boy returned, and said the painter had "no orders to tip it with green."

Thereupon Toole appealed to the guard, who was an exceptionally anxious-looking person.

"It is always a difficult thing," Toole said to

MR. TOOLE AND THE STATION-MASTER—"TIP IT WITH GREEN."

him, with a grave face, "to make alterations when you settle the colour of a particular style of decoration; but the directors have come to the conclusion that the scroll-work round the pillars is too plain,—wants variety; and they have decided to have it tipped with green. I wish you would tell the painter there to tip it with green."

"Well," said the guard, "I've no time to spare, sir, but I'll just speak to the station-master." Before Toole could interpose, the guard rushed to the other end of the platform and sent the station-master, a courteous and imposing-looking official, to our carriage.

I was beginning to laugh, and to wonder how my friend would get out of this unexpected difficulty.

"Keep your countenance," he said, "it's all right."

The station-master came up.

"Oh, about the painting of the station?" said Toole.

"Yes, sir; what is it?"

"Well, we had a meeting yesterday, and we think it would be wise to relieve the decoration with a little green. You see it's rather monotonous, that blue and magenta; and although the contract has been given out, and actually begun, we reconsidered it yesterday on good advice—I was speaking to the inspector—and we have had a good deal of—of—of talk about it. A little thing makes such a difference, doesn't it?"

"Well, it does," said the station-master.

" And we thought that if a little orange or green were introduced into the filagree work on the pillars—it would be an improvement. Of course you can never quite tell what the effect will be until you see a thing, but I am quite sure it would be better if it was tipped with green. Will you be good enough to tell the man there who is at work—an excellent man, knows his business, I'm sure—will you just tell him to *tip it with green ?* "

" Certainly," said the station-master, going off with an official stride to the painter. We watched the encounter, noting the action of the station-master, who was evidently explaining Toole's views.

The painter paused for a moment or two in his work and made some response to the station-master, who returned to us.

" Well," said Toole, " what does he say ? "

" He says the foreman of the works is away just now, gone to his dinner, and he has no orders to introduce any other colour ; but he will speak to the foreman about it."

" Ah," said Toole, " thank you very much. Shall you see the foreman of the works this afternoon ? "

" Yes, sir, I shall."

" Well, now, will you be good enough to jog

his memory about it; and tell him we wish it to be tipped with green."

" I will, sir, certainly," said the station-master.

The train moved quietly out of the station and brought us alongside the painter. As we passed him, Toole, with a broad grin on his face, called out, " Hi ! you there ! painter ! "

The man turned round a little angrily.

" *Tip it with green !* " said Toole.

The painter laid down his brush, looked a trifle savage, then gradually relapsed into a broad grin, and waved his brush at us, as he realized the situation and caught on the artificial breeze created by the passing train Toole's parting words : " *Tip it with green !* " [1]

[1] Mr. H. Werner writes to the *Newcastle Weekly Chronicle* describing another railway incident :—" Mr. Toole was travelling a short time ago on the Great Eastern line from Ipswich to Cambridge. The train was a slow one, and the journey, in consequence, very tedious. When Bury St. Edmund's was reached, the comedian was thoroughly wearied out by the length of time the train was delayed at the station. Calling a porter, he asked in a very bland manner for the station-master, who, all politeness, bustled up to the door of the carriage in which sat Mr. Toole, looking as solemn as a judge. ' What is it, sir ? ' asked the official. ' At what time is the funeral to take place ? ' inquired Mr. Toole. ' Funeral, sir ? Whose funeral ? ' inquired the now wondering station-master. ' Whose funeral ! ' continued Mr. Toole ; ' why, have we not come to Bury St. Edmund's ? ' Exit station-master in a huff."

II.

THIS little jest at the expense of the York station-master set us both recalling the practical jokes of Sothern,[2] some of which are characterized by a

---

[2] " My theatrical recollections of New York include, at Laura Keene's, the production of a play destined to attain celebrity as *Our American Cousin*, in which I saw Sothern act 'Lord Dundreary' for the very first time in his life ; and some years afterwards, when we first met at the Theatre Royal, Dublin, I gave him a copy of the original play-bill which I chanced to have kept.   Jefferson, since world-famous as 'Rip Van Winkle,' was the 'Asa Trenchard.'   The whole performance was a very different one from that presented later at the Haymarket ; but beyond all dispute, it was 'Dundreary' who made the play, always a very bad one, although through Sothern it enjoyed the then greatest run on record.   Sothern, at the reading of the piece, refused his part, and only on being given *carte blanche* to 'write it up' and do with it what he pleased, consented to appear in it.   The odd stammer and eccentric walk which he introduced he had previously tried with success in small Canadian towns, where he began his Western career as 'Sir Frederick Blount' in *Money ;* its inspiration being really due to some funny antics of a nigger troupe known as Bryant's Min-strels.   The long claret-coloured Noah's Ark coat which he wore on the first night he borrowed from Dion Boucicault, who was then acting at Niblo's ; this dress was only once changed throughout the comedy, and then for a costume which would not have disgraced Wright in an old Adelphi farce—the coal-black whiskers were an exaggeration of the peg-top fashion then the rage, which also governed largely the cut of trousers and coat-sleeves.   There was not for a long time any Brother Sam's letter or any allusion to that fraternal personage.   The part grew slowly bit by bit, and instead of being exaggerated

droll humour. As previously suggested, Sothern's fooling now and then overstepped the line of good taste, but it was always instinct with a keen sense of the dramatic effect of humorous incongruity.

Mrs. John Wood told me the following story of Sothern. They were both playing at Birmingham. She met him accidentally in the neighbourhood of New Street. They were near an ironmonger's shop, when he shook hands with her and bade her good morning.

"Would you mind going in here with me? I want to make a little purchase," he said.

She accompanied him.

He went up to the counter and said, " I want Macaulay's ' History of England.' "

The assistant said, " We do not sell books, sir ; this is an ironmonger's shop."

" Well, I'm not particular," said Sothern, pretending to be deaf. " I don't care whether it is bound in calf or Russia."

" But this is not a bookseller's," shouted the assistant.

into an impossibility, as it might have been by an inferior actor, was, in fact, refined nightly in action and costume with the judgment and painstaking labour which always characterized this admirable comedian, of whom I shall hope later on to speak."—Mr. Bancroft's Narrative, in " Mr. and Mrs. Bancroft on and off the Stage."

" All right," said Sothern. " Wrap it up neatly. I want to have it sent down to the hotel. It's for a present I wish to make to a relative. Put it up nicely."

" We don't keep it," shouted the assistant,

MRS. JOHN WOOD.
(*From an American photograph.*)

getting red in the face ; while Mrs. Wood stepped aside and took a chair in another part of the shop, almost overcome with suppressed laughter at the cheerful, frank expression of Sothern's face, and the mad, puzzled look of the shopkeeper's assistant.

" Do it up as if it were for your own mother.

I don't want anything better than that," said Sothern.   " I would like to write my name on the fly-leaf."

"Sir," bawled the assistant at the top of his voice, "can't you see we do not keep books."

"Very well," said Sothern, quite undisturbed at the emotion he was creating, " I will wait for it."

Under the impression that his customer was either stone-deaf or a lunatic, the assistant bounced off to the further end of the shop, and asked his master to come. " I can do nothing with him: I think he must be off his head." Whereupon the principal marched up to the spot where Sothern was standing, and asked very loudly, "What is it, sir!   What do you desire ? "

" I want to buy a file," says Sothern, quietly ; " a plain file, about four or five inches in length."

" Certainly," said the principal, with a withering look at his assistant, and producing at once the article which had been asked for.

" Are you ready ? " said Sothern to Mrs. Wood. She was not as ready as usual.

III.

" One of the most elaborate of Sothern's jokes, said Toole, " was the little affair he arranged for the improvement of Mr. Philip Lee's knowledge of American life. Lee, as you know, was the husband of Miss Neilson. When first he went to America with his wife, he frequently remarked that New York didn't seem to him any more uncivilized than London. He had heard a great deal of the wild doings of the American cities. Mr. Sothern, indeed, had particularly cautioned him in regard to New York. He had not exactly described Central Park to him as a prairie abounding with wild game, but he had depicted to him the possible dangers which always beset a stranger in the streets of New York.

"Mr. Lee, at a little supper party, told Sothern he believed he had been chaffing him : he didn't think people went about armed in New York, nor did he see the possibilities of danger against which he had been warned.

"Sothern, in reply, said of course Lee was in very good society, had been introduced to good clubs and good people, and was not in the way of seeing what was called 'American life ;' but it was, nevertheless, a common practice for men to shoot at each other over dinner ; get up sudden quarrels, and have fights quite as tragic as were frequently reported in 'the far West.' Would he care to see a little New York life ? He and his friend Florence would like to introduce him to a few remarkable characters. Lee accepted the invitation with pleasure.

" A dinner was arranged at a down-town restaurant, the guests specially invited and rehearsed. They consisted of one or two actors and a couple of leading minstrels of the Moore and Burgess class, who were both dressed and armed for the parts they had to play. When they sat down to dinner, one of these men drew from the back of his collar a formidable bowie-knife and laid it beside his plate; the other took out a six-shooter in an ordinary way and placed it on his right hand. One of the actors spoke of having just come off an awkward journey, and deposited what he called a bull-dozer beneath his chair. There was a good deal of noisy discussion over dinner, particularly between Mr. Florence and the gentleman who had just come off the awkward journey. The *menu* having been pretty well exhausted, Florence reached over towards the traveller for the pepper-box; whereupon the awkward customer, leaping to his feet, said, ' Put that pepper-box down ! '

" Florence made a scoffing remark : whereupon the other guest stooped for his revolver, and in an instant Florence, drawing a bowie-knife, leaped across the table to the attack ; whereupon there was a general rising. The gas went out ;

several pistol-shots were fired; there was a great crash of chairs and plates, and evidently a most tragic scene was being enacted in the dark.

" In the midst of it, however, most of the guests disappeared; and when the waiters came in, Mr. Lee was found under the table, unhurt, but in a state of considerable nervous exhaustion, and ready, it is said, to get out of that ' cussed country' forthwith."

IV.

FLORENCE, going home late one night, found upon his dining-room table a very tender note in a lady's handwriting. The signature was unknown to him, and after carefully considering the epistle, he came to the conclusion that his friend Sothern was the author of it. Mrs. Florence had fortunately retired before its arrival. Florence immediately wrote, and despatched by a messenger —one of the pleasant facilities for communication you have in New York—a furious letter to Sothern, from whose persecution, as he regarded it, in another matter, he was keenly suffering at the moment.

" Your conduct," he wrote, " is neither that of an actor nor a gentleman."

In the morning he regretted the letter he had

written ; but the messenger-boys of New York are almost as swift as the telegraph. His letter had been duly received.

A few weeks afterwards Florence met Sothern in Union Square.

" How d'you do, Florence ? " said Sothern· " You're quite a stranger."

"That's how I have been feeling," said Florence. " Ever since I wrote that letter to you I concluded it would put an end to our friendship."

" That letter—what letter ? Oh, yes, I remember: something about neither an actor nor a gentleman ? But there was no name at the bottom ; I remember now ; so guessing it was intended for Boucicault, I re-directed it and sent it on." [3]

[3] There is a capital story of Florence—an episode of the actor's boyish days in "Henry Irving's Impressions of America," which is worth remembering. Florence was a very young man, a boy, in fact, and was filling one of his first engagements on any stage at the Bowery Theatre. A girl about his own age (who is now a wife, and a woman of position in New York) in the company, was his first love. His adoration was mingled with the most gallant respect. Their salaries were about from ten to twelve dollars each a week. For a time they only played in the first piece ; for in those days two plays a night were more popular on the American stage than they are now. One evening, at about nine o'clock, after pulling himself together for so daring an effort in his course of court ship, he asked her if she would go to an adjacent restaurant and take something to eat. The house was kept by a person

V.

"You knew Johnnie Clarke, of course," said
Toole, after a long pause, during which time the

MR. JOHN CLARKE.

North-Eastern train had been running along at

of the name of Shields, or Shiells. The supper-room was
arranged something after the manner of the old London
coffee-houses. It had compartments divided off from each
other. Into one of these Florence escorted his sweetheart.
He asked her what she would take. After some hesitation,
and a good deal of blushing (more probably on his part than
hers), she said oyster-stew and lemonade. He concluded to
have the same—an incongruous mixture, perhaps ; but they
were boy and girl. Florence was more than once on the eve
of declaring his undying passion and asking her to name the

the rate of sixty miles an hour through pleasant, restful scenery.

day. Presently, supper being ended, they rose to go, and Florence discovered that he had come away without his purse, or rather, his pocket-book, as they call it here. He explained to the Irish waiter (and Florence I suspect is himself of Irish descent), who cut him short by saying, "Money? Oh, that won't do; you're not going to damage the moral character of the house, bringing of your girls here, and then saying you can't pay the bill." "How dare you, sir!" exclaimed Florence, the girl shrinking back. "Dare! Oh, bedad, if you put that in the way I'll just give you a piece of my mind;" and he did. It was a dirty piece, which hurt the poor young fellow. "Take me to your master," he said. The girl was crying; Florence was heartbroken. The master was not less rude than the man. "Very well," said the boy; "here's my watch and ring. I will call and redeem them in the morning with the money. I am a member of the Bowery company, and I will ask the manager to call and see you also. Your conduct is shameful." "By heaven, it is," exclaimed a stranger, who, with some others, was smoking near the desk of the clerk or landlord. "It is infamous, cannot you understand that this young gentleman is a good, honest young fellow? ——, you ought to apologize to him, and kick that waiter-fellow out. Don't frown at me, sir. Give the young gentleman his watch and ring. Here is a fifty-dollar bill; take what he owes, and give me the change." The stranger was a well-dressed gentleman, with white hair; not old, but of venerable appearance. They all went out together—Florence, the young lady, and their benefactor. As they stepped into the street, Florence said, "I cannot sufficiently thank you, sir. Where shall I call and leave the money for you?" "Oh, don't trouble yourself about it," said the benevolent gentleman; "your surly friend won't make much out of the transaction,—it was a counterfeit bill that he changed for me."

" Oh, yes," I said, " a clever, eccentric come-dian." [4]

[4] " Both the play-going public, who have lost the services of an admirable comedian, and the theatrical profession, who will miss the companionship of a widely-esteemed friend, must receive with the deepest regret the intelligence that this deservedly popular actor is no longer among us.   Since the death of his wife Mr. John Clarke had greatly suffered in health, and during the last two months his illness, arising from a deeply-seated affection of the lungs, increased to such an extent that but small hope could be entertained of his ultimate recovery. For some days past those who had called to see him had brought back reports of increasing fits of coughing and rapidly diminishing strength ; and on Thursday morning, at half-past eight, he expired, at his residence, 15, Torriano Avenue, Camden Road.   His age was about fifty.   In early life Mr. John Clarke showed a strong predilection for the stage, and eventually he gave up a photographic establishment in Farringdon Street, which he had opened with some prospect of success, and went as ' general utility' to serve country theatres in succession.   His first appearance before a London audience was in January, 1852, at the Strand Theatre, then under the management of Mr Allcroft.   The part he played was ' Master Toby,' in Wilkins's play of *Civilization*.   During a speculative management at Drury Lane he made a further trial of his abilities, appearing on October 7th, 1852, as ' Fathom,' in *The Hunchback*, but, the season only lasting a few nights, he returned to the provinces, and reappeared in September, 1855, at the Strand, taking the position of principal comedian, and making a notable hit, as ' Ikey, the Jew,' in Mr. Leicester Buckingham's burlesque of *Belphegor*, produced in September, 1856.   At Christmas, 1857, he was engaged by Mr. E. T. Smith, for Drury Lane, and appeared as ' Old Proverb,' in the pantomime of *Little Jack Horner*.   Returning to the Strand in 1858, when Miss Swanborough had raised the theatre to more

" The same!" exclaimed my genial companion in a tragic tone. " Poor Johnnie, he was a curious little chap. He played 'Ikey, the Jew,' in *Belphegor.* His 'Isaac' in the burlesque of *The Maid and the Magpie;* his 'Quasimodo' in *Esmeralda;* and 'Beauséant,' in the burlesque of *The Lady of Lyons,* were all excellent.

importance than it had previously acquired, Mr. John Clarke established himself as a prominent member of a really excellent company, and at this establishment he remained several years, identifying himself with a memorable series of characters in the extravaganzas written by Francis Talfourd and H. J. Byron, and making a great hit in such pieces as *The Last of the Pigtails, The Bonny Fishwife,* and *The Goose with the Golden Eggs.* In the burlesque parts of ' Isaac,' in *The Maid and the Magpie;* ' Varney,' in *Kenilworth;* ' Quasimodo, in *Esmeralda;* 'Beauseant,' in *The Lady of Lyons;* and ' Gesler,' in *William Tell,* his memory will be long preserved by those who were frequenters of the theatre during the brightest period of its prosperity. As a grotesque singer and dancer he had rare advantages, and his embodiments were always characterized by singular care bestowed on what is technically called ' the making-up.' Subsequently he accepted an engagement with Mr. Benjamin Webster, at the Adelphi, joined the Olympic company and made a marked impression as ' Quilp;' acted for some time at the Globe Theatre; played at Covent Garden during the Christmas season, when *The Babes in the Wood* was produced; for two years he was prominently associated with the Prince of Wales's Theatre; and finally appeared at the Criterion, where he performed with great success in several new pieces, and in the revival of *The Porter's Knot.* In 1873 Mr. John Clarke married the clever actress, Miss Teresa Furtado, who expired at the early age of thirty-two, August 9th, 1877."—The *Era,* February 20th, 1879.

"He was quite a character in his way; touchy, simple-minded, thought himself rather knowing, but was very transparent in his foibles. His house was a sort of half-way house in Park Village, between the Strand and Haverstock Hill. Andrew Halliday, Billington, Charles Dickens, jun., and myself, and some other friends would occasionally drive home together, and drop Johnnie on the way. We always had a bit of fun with him. He was very earnest about his acting, and had a great belief in himself. If it was moderately early, we would manage to pay him a compliment or two, and he would invite us in.

"Then one of us would remark that Webster's 'Triplet' or Dillon's 'Belphegor' were wonderful histrionic studies; or that Robson in *The Porter's Knot* would be a living memory when we were all gone; and, to get nearer home, we would mention some low comedian or character-actor who had been sustaining some part in Clarke's line.

"Clarke would interrupt us with a suggestion that he had done something also in that way; but we would carefully avoid all reference to him; and all of a sudden, unable to bear it any longer, he would say, 'Well, boys, I am sorry I can't invite you to have a parting drink; whisky's locked up; must say good-night;' and he would lead the way to the door. But as we had come for the purpose of remaining a little while, and taking that parting drink, Halliday would lay his hand on Clarke's shoulder and say, ' But your " Ikey, the Jew," Johnny, will be hard to beat,' and I would add, ' But what do you say of his " Quilp " ? '

" He would melt under this, and say, ' Oh, well, I think " Quilp " was not so bad. Don't go, boys ; stay and have a drink. What's your hurry ? It isn't late.'

" And we would all return pleasantly to his quaint little dining-room, and spend the remainder of the evening.

"Clarke married Miss Furtado, a bright, pretty, clever actress. When she was playing ' Esmeralda,' he took down a goat for her on the first evening. I remember his telling me that he had a regular fight with it in the cab. He thought it would have butted him to death. With assistance, however, he succeeded in landing the attraction at the theatre, with what result I don't remember."

VI.

Apropos of these reminiscences of Clarke, Toole said, " The jealousies in the profession of the stage are, I suppose, not more serious than the jealousies in other walks of life ; but they are sometimes more inconvenient, if not more amusing.

" Years ago at Newcastle-on-Tyne,[5] when I was on tour with *Dot* and other attractive plays, Irving

[5] " H. W. R." writes as follows to the *Newcastle Daily Chronicle* :—" I have been much interested in Mr. Toole's ' Reminiscences,' and this week's contribution reminds me of some circumstances which occurred on the occasion of the comedian's visit to Newcastle in 1870, when he got himself into rather an awkward scrape. Much to my disappointment, Mr. Toole has not mentioned it, though even his multitudinous experiences of scrapes can hardly have obliterated the New-castle one from his memory.

" He had come down to fulfil a week's engagement at the Tyne Theatre. For a fortnight or three weeks before, the hoardings and bill-posting stations in the town had been pla-carded with large diamond-shaped bills with deep blue or red borders, bearing one word. I have forgotten what the word was, but we will say it was ' Arachne.' Preliminary advertise-ments of that sort were not so common then as they have been since. Curiosity was aroused, and every one was on the tip-toe of expectation as to the sequel. On the Quayside, and wherever young men did congregate, it became a password, and many a good joke resulted therefrom. Two or three days after Mr. Toole's arrival the people were surprised one morn-ing to see a fresh set of bills out. Printed at the top, in large letters, was the mystic word, ' Arachne,' and below, ' Toole's benefit at the Tyne Theatre to-night.'

" That night the popular comedian had a bumper. At the close of the performance, in obedience to the vociferous applause of the immense audience, Mr. Toole came before the curtain. After thanking them for the reception they had given him, he said he was sorry to tell them that he had got into serious trouble. He came to the town and found the public mind in a state of tension, and in order to relieve them of their suspense he simply appropriated the mysterious ' ad.' He had been threatened with all sorts of pains and penalties, but if the

playing ' John Peerybingle ' and Brough ' Tackleton,' we were considerably upset one evening after
the second act of *Dot*, with the announcement that
the lady who played ' Bertha, the Blind Girl,' had
been taken suddenly ill, and could not finish the
piece.   She lay in her dressing-room in a dead
faint, and although at the outset of her illness she
had spoken and said she could not go on again,
nothing now had any effect upon her.   We sent
for a doctor, and in the meantime set about trying
to fill her place.   The part ought to have been
understudied, but it was not ; there was a lady in
the company who was not playing that night ; she
happened to be in front with her husband ; she
was sent for.   I asked her to go on for ' Bertha,'
and said I would give her the words as we went
along.   In the first place she said nothing would
induce her to do anything for the lady who was
ill ; but there was nothing in the world she would
not do for me.

" At the same time, she would consent to do
nothing but read the part.   I pointed out to her
how absurd it would be for a blind girl to read a
part.   Irving, in a quiet way, said it would certainly be a novelty.   However, she was obdurate,

public of Newcastle thought he had wronged them, he would
be glad to come down and play for the benefit of the Infirmary.
He retired amidst the most enthusiastic applause."

and Irving made the announcement to the audience that the lady who had played the blind girl had been taken suddenly ill; and under the circumstances Miss So-and-so had kindly consented to read the part. The audience applauded, and seemed quite satisfied. Irving came from the front of the curtain remarking that it was, to use a classic phrase, 'a rum go;' but it was a much rummer go than any of us foresaw.

"Under treatment the fainting lady came round, and the moment she learned that her rival was going on in her place, she leaped to her feet and emphatically said, 'Never, never!'

"I was on the stage as 'Caleb Plummer,' and of course knew nothing of this, but when the time arrived for the pathetic entrance of the girl to myself and 'Dot,' I heard quite a disturbance at the wing; the audience heard it too.

"'You shall not go on.' 'I must.' 'You shall not, I say!' 'But I have been announced.' 'I don't care; I am better, and I am going on!'

"Then there was something like a scuffle, and the original blind girl, for whose illness we had apologized, came bounding on with a look of defiance in her very widely-opened eyes. The audience laughed heartily and applauded vociferously, and when the baggage began to speak I believe she winked at the house, as much as to say, 'They don't get over me;' and the play went on. I need not say the spirit and intention of the scene was spoiled; but the audience was very good, and after all it was better to play the scene anyhow than have the blind girl read it. And as I said, although 'the good Samaritan' would do anything for me, she would not for any one in the world walk on for a part she did not know without the book, though she had seen it played scores of times."

VII.

IRVING tells a capital story of Toole. I heard him narrate it over an American dinner-table, by way of showing that our cousins do not entirely monopolize the instinct of advertising. He has since then contributed it as " a light fantastic tale " to the *Clover Leaves* in America, " not only because it exhibits an interesting trait in my old friend's character, but also because it deserves to be an imperishable illustration of English manners in an American volume, to which in the course of the next five hundred years the historian of our present civilization will naturally turn for his most instructive facts." This is the story :—

" A vast amount of years ago—it must be fully fourteen—I was playing in Byron's drama, *Uncle*

Dick's Darling, at the Gaiety Theatre, in London. My dear old friend, J. L. Toole, was the bright particular star of that entertainment, and Adelaide Neilson was the 'Darling.' Now, my friend Toole, amongst many brilliant qualities, has a notable faculty for business, and in the invention of captivating posters and insinuating handbills he had at that time no equal. Pray don't think he cares for such arts now, for he long ago discovered their vanity, when after playing for a week in a certain place he met the local bill-printer, to whom he had paid a lot of money, and who greeted him with: 'Hallo, Mr. Toole! How long have you been here?' Still, before this awakening his activity in advertising was extreme. One of his rivals, an eminent tragedian, was once much moved when leaving a town to find his posters covered with the announcement: 'Toole is coming;' and the climax of torment was reached when, going to bed that night, he found this stimulating legend pinned on his pillow.

"Well, my indefatigable friend was not content with playing superbly in *Uncle Dick's Darling*. He busied himself with all manner of devices to popularize the performance. He never went anywhere without a bundle of labels in his pocket, and if he happened to be in a church or a police-court, or any other place of fashionable resort, he was sure to leave behind him a touching memento sticking in some prominent place, to the effect that J. L. Toole was to be seen at the Gaiety Theatre in *Uncle Dick's Darling* every evening. And I have lately been credibly informed that one of these labels pleasantly adorns the tomb of the Pharoahs.

"About this time died William Brough, one of the well-known brothers who did so much good work for the stage and periodical literature. No doubt you have read the genial recollections of them in Edmund Yates's 'Reminiscences.' To poor William Brough's funeral, in a cemetery a little way out of London, Toole and I repaired one cold and drizzly afternoon—just the kind of day when the gloomy reminder that we are all mortal becomes most oppressive. We saw our dead friend laid in the earth, and as we turned away, wondering whose scene with the grave-digger would come next, the prosaic suggestion was made that perhaps some degree of physical comfort might be got out of a little hot brandy-and-water. This idea was embraced with alacrity; and while we were thus consoling ourselves in a neighbouring inn, our attention was attracted by a crowd surrounding an object lying in the gutter. My friend's fertile brain was awake at once; so we quickly made our way to the spot, and found that some too-thirsty soul, tempted by a barrel of spirits which had burst in the street, had drunk not wisely but too well.   The crowd stood gazing at the body in a helpless way, but my companion knew his cue at once.   Pushing his way through the throng, followed by me, his admiring assistant, and suggesting that he was a doctor, he knelt beside the fallen reveler, whose shirt-collar he unbuttoned, felt his pulse, laid his hand on his heart, and performed with impressive accuracy the whole professional routine.   The people watched the process with sympathy and confidence, and when my friend said, ' It's not very serious, I can soon put him right again,' there was a hum of approval and admiration.   Feeling in one of his pockets, the ' doctor ' took out something, which he applied to the patient's forehead.   From another pocket he took something else, and applied it to one cheek, while a third pocket yielded a further medicament for the other cheek.   Then looking round with a thoughtful and abstracted air, one hand covering the face of the patient, with the other he removed a cap from the head of a gaping and bewildered boy, and dextrously placed it on the beplastered visage of the prostrate Briton.

" ' Now,' said he triumphantly, ' leave him alone for five minutes, and " Richard's himself again." '

" We then withdrew, and with some celerity

jumped into a cab, followed with a suppressed
cheer.   But we had not proceeded far when a yell
of execration broke upon our ears ; for the impatient crowd had found that the object of their
commiseration was no less a person than ' *Uncle
Dick's Darling*, Gaiety Theatre, every evening.' "

VIII.

AT Whitby we encountered a cab-driver, who in
an unconscious stupid kind of way proved to be
more than a match for us.   To begin with he was
a dolt of the most unpromising character.   He
drove us to wrong places and made silly mistakes
in regard to our instructions.   At the close he
developed a cunning mendacity.

In the midst of one of his gravest errors I said
to him, " You don't seem to know anything at all
about Whitby.   Where are you going to drive to
now ? "

" Well," he said, " I was agoing round to the
pier."

" I said the post-office."

" Very well, sir," he said.

Whereupon Toole remarked, " My friend says
you don't know anything at all about Whitby."

" Oh, yes, I do, sir ; I know all about Whitby."

" Very well, then, perhaps you can tell me whether Mr. Joheronfg is still living in Whitby ? "

" Yes, sir ; he is."

" What, up there on the cliffs ? "

" Yes, sir."

" I thought," continued Toole, " he had left the town when his little boy hurt his finger in that accident.   But I am glad to hear he is still here."

" Oh, yes ; he still lives here."

" Do you remember the accident ? "

" Oh, yes, sir."

" Was it a black pony ? "

" It was, sir."

" Didn't hurt him very much ? "

" No; sir."

" Only his finger ? "

" No, sir."

" Do the Jorkinses still live at the old house ? "

" I believe they does, sir."

" Mrs. Jorkins and the family ? "

" Yes, sir."

" Quite right," said Toole.   " Very well.   Drive on to the post-office.   You evidently do know all about Whitby."

" Yes, sir.   I've lived here all my life.   I knows Whitby as well as most."

" Very well.   Drive to the post-office."

IX.

THAT night after the play we supped at the hotel with George Loveday, whom Toole kept in a continuous chuckle over our adventures at York.

It is always the humorous or the pathetic aspect of an incident that takes Toole's fancy, rarely the simply dramatic. He does not see things from their acting point of view as Irving does: he is not continually placing events and characters on the stage as Irving is, decorating them with stage effects, mounting and lighting them and playing them in imagination. Occurrences that are funny or sad strike Toole as current incidents, move him pathetically or excite into activity his natural love of fun. He may unconsciously store away the results, and they may crop up in his work; but in the case of the actor who has done so much as Irving for the poetical drama, and who has so keen a sense of what is strong and gloomy and awe-inspiring in stage stories, there is a continually watchful eye upon nature for poetic and dramatic suggestions, not alone as regards individual characterization, but in connection with dramatic catastrophe and theatrical effect. Then again, Toole is a born *raconteur*. He finds pleasure in the narration of funny things that have struck him during the day, odd incidents of travel, curious details in regard to his business. His friend

SUPPER AND STORIES AT WHITBY.

Irving is also an excellent story-teller, but the gift is not spontaneous with him as with Toole. His thoughts are more engaged in the shaping of future enterprises than with the affairs of the moment.   No one admires Toole's gift of fun and humorous narrative more than Irving.

I am tempted into these passing reflections by the remembrance of a previous visit to Whitby, and of the first night of my stay with Irving at this little Yorkshire sea-port.   It was autumn then, as on the present occasion, somewhat stormy, too, and cold.   But instead of sitting indoors and re-enacting the fun of the day, and recalling other humorous events, we strolled out into the night when Whitby was a-bed, and listened to the warning bell that boomed in the moaning waters off the coast ; a gloomy yet fascinating sound at night with the sea in darkness—only a strange void and blackness to tell us that it was writhing and tossing at our feet, and the bell moaning of rocks or shoals or other hidden dangers, upon which in the olden days many a stalwart mariner had come to grief, with its funereal music in his ears.   We talked of what might have happened, what does happen, every day in stormy seas ; of the ballad of the Inchcape rock ; of the marvellous tale of the shipwreck of the *Hooker*, as told by Victor Hugo ; the snow-storm, the philosopher, and " the bell of the abyss."

Irving was at this time in the midst of negotiations for his first visit to America, wondering what the great Atlantic sea was like, how the

Americans would accept his art, how he would like his Transatlantic audiences. It is wonderful what a tremendous event our first trip to America seems to all of us ; how small a matter our second voyage. Now that Toole and I were here on the Yorkshire coast together for the first time, letting the sea-bell toll at its own sweet will without comment or attention, Irving was away in the United States on his second professional tour ; and by the time these words are printed he will have visited the country a third and fourth time for pleasure and for business.

X.

"Too much travelling for me," remarks Toole, "in the United States. A great country, no doubt, grand mountains and rivers, cities nearly all alike, and I don't see the advantage of size and magnificent distances which they are rather fond of talking about. It seems to me we have a pull in that matter, as I did not hesitate to tell them. Surely, as a matter of business convenience, to say nothing of keeping up personal friendships, it is a mistake to have the leading cities of a nation so far apart as they are in America. I can run to Manchester from London in four hours ; it takes about thirty-six to get to Chicago from New York; it is only a comfortable day's trip, with a timely stoppage for dinner *en route*, between the Metropolis and Glasgow; it takes more than a week to get from New York to San Francisco. I think our arrangement is best; a tight little island, the theatres all over the land, within easy distance from each other and from London. I liked a lot of what I saw in America, and I have some dear kind friends there, but the travelling, the long distances, the heated railway-cars! Well, give me old England!"

"And tip it with green," remarked Loveday, beginning to laugh afresh over the comedy of the railway-station.

Toole's manner is irresistible. If anybody had known him long enough to grow tired of his fun it was Loveday; he was not demonstrative in his mirth, his laugh was occasionally hearty, but as a rule it consisted of a chuckle and a sympathetic glance at his fellow-listeners. "And to me," said Loveday, *entre nous*, "he is always fresh and humorous, and his energy is, after all these years, a constant surprise. What astonishes me," continued Loveday, "is that when Johnny said, 'Tip it with green,' the station-master did not discover the joke."

"And it was that which most surprised me," I

said; "but Toole was so intensely earnest, seemed so anxious to save the Company's money and the painter's time that any one might have been deceived. I only hope the station-master will enjoy the joke as much as we do. It had occurred to me that when the official in his fine uniform came up to the carriage, Toole would make some pleasant remark and let the matter drop. The boldness of attempting to trifle with so distinguished a person deserved success; failure must have been ignominious."

"It will amuse Irving," said Toole; "I don't know any one who enjoys a joke so much or so long. By the way, you want me to tell you some things about Irving;" then, turning to Loveday, he said, "Hatton is really writing those remarkable reminiscences after all."

Loveday smiled incredulously.

"I am making notes all the time—have come to stay a week with you for that especial purpose," I said.

"Yes," said Loveday, smiling, "I have heard of other fellows coming down to visit us for a day or two, in order to do a little quiet literary work. We shall see."

Later, however, the genial cynic confessed he thought I had done "some good work on the book," and that the York adventures were "first rate." I wonder if he was right, poor fellow, in this pleasant expression of opinion. The reader knows; and in due course I shall probably be as wise as the reader.

V.

COMBINING BUSINESS WITH PLEASURE.

At Robin Hood's Bay—On certain military pickles—Stories of Compton—With Macready—A grim joke—" Business is business "—The pathetic parting of King and Brooke—" Macreadiana "—Miss Kelly at Feltham—" Chestnuts " and story-tellers—An incident of Sackville Street—The " Dodger's " wardrobe and the dealer in cast-off garments —A Belfast incident—Toole and the tailor—Mr. Percy Fitzgerald's " Irvingiana."

I.

WE spent three quiet, pleasant days at Whitby. The theatre stands upon a terrace by the sea. In the daytime we took long drives over the Yorkshire moors. At night my host would slip a coat over his theatrical costume and join me in a lounge between the acts. *The Serious Family* more particularly enabled him to do this. I smoked; he talked; it was lovely weather. The theatre emptied itself for ten minutes between the pieces. The audience—smoking, flirting, chatting—little thought my companion was " Mr. Spriggins " or " Mr. Sleek," as the case might be. Toole treated

the engagement as a real holiday. He was over-
joyed at getting back to the footlights. Not quite
himself physically, he was nevertheless cheerful as

MR. TOOLE AS "MR. SLEEK" IN "THE SERIOUS FAMILY."

ever, and he improved in health every day. "I
think I should die," he said, "if I were cut off
from work." Yes, he called it work. There are
unsophisticated people who think acting is play,

and I fear these Reminiscences may tend to confirm them in that opinion.

One day we drove to Robin Hood's Bay. At the local tavern there, with its tea-garden arrangement, near the sea, we proposed to lunch.

"What can we have to eat?" Toole asked.

"We have a joint of cold lamb, sir," said the waiter.

"Anything else?"

"Cold ham, sir, and there are eggs."

"Any salad?"

"No, sir; pickles, very good pickles."

"Whose pickles?"

"Captain White's pickles?"

"Very well," said Toole; "cold lamb and Captain White's pickles."

"Funny the pickles should be Captain White's," said Toole, "because I was leading up to pickles, the Captain's in particular. I wanted to tell you about White's pickles, whether the Robin Hood pickles were dignified with his brand, or were only Crosse and Blackwell's, or Batty's, or anybody else's. Not long ago I was stranded at an out-of-the-way inn, waiting for Loveday, and, after a cold bit of supper, I found myself dramatizing, as you call it, a bottle of Captain White's pickles. I began wondering when he had thought of this concoction to which he had given his name. Had he been inspired with the recipe on the field of battle? Why 'Captain White's pickles'? Had the method of mixing dawned upon him while riding to the front, sword in hand, at the head of his troops; or, the advance being ordered, had he exclaimed, 'Oh, Pickles!' before seeking convenient shelter from the foe? I saw Captain White in all kinds of heroic positions, but I turned them all into ridicule. Then I wondered if the soldiers of his company helped him to put the pickles into the bottles and stick the labels on. I tried to imagine his lieutenants and subalterns, in full-dress uniform, occupied in the work of preparing the pickles, bottling them, labelling them, packing them up and sending them off in great parcels by train. If I had been a comic writer, I believe I should have done something for *Punch* about Captain White's pickles. In that case I suppose Burnand would have taken his revenge by playing 'Spriggins' or 'Chawles'; and I am not so sure that he would not have had the best of it.

Then, with a sudden transition from gaiety to gravity, he exclaimed, "Oh, here's an incident for the Reminiscences! I don't know why I think of it at the moment, because it is not in the least relevant to Burnand, or to *Punch*, or to pickles."

"Perhaps that is the reason why," I suggested.

"And yet it has something to do with eating.

You knew Compton—a capital comedian—a quaint, dry style.   He had a very dry humour, and was a most agreeable fellow.   I remember dining with him at Sir Henry Thompson's ; Sothern was one of the company.   After dinner Compton was unusually quiet.

" 'You seem to be of a reflective turn of mind this evening,' said our excellent host.

" 'Yes,' said Compton, pointing to a lovely study of feminine beauty upon the wall opposite, 'you have given me something which encourages thought.   I have been regretting my lost youth, Sir Henry, and trying to realize the severity of the temptation of St. Anthony.'

" But this is the story of Compton that occurred to me.   He had rather a clerical air ; might well have been mistaken for an unostentatious curate, as in fact he was mistaken.   It was at a country town, where a clerical meeting was being held ; one of those occasional gatherings when the clergy dine at the leading hotel of the place.   Compton was passing through the town, and hoped to find an ordinary at the hotel.

" 'The bishop and the clergy of the diocese are just about sitting down to dinner,' said the headwaiter, ' and I believe they would be glad to have you join them.   I know they have invited a travelling stranger to do so before now upon an occasion of this kind. I will ask permission, if you will allow me ; ' and before Compton had time to say yes or no, he was informed that the bishop would be very glad if he would partake of the feast. Dinner was being served and Compton was hungry ; he entered the dining-hall. The bishop bowed to him, and room was made for him not far from the presiding clergyman, who, looking towards Compton, said,—

" ' Will our stranger guest say grace ? '

" Compton was staggered for a moment, all the grace he knew slipping at once straight out of his memory. Like myself, he was a church-goer ; and in the emergency a familiar passage from the Prayer Book occurred to him as not unsuitable to the occasion, and the clergy accepted the new form of grace as a bit of clerical eccentricity.

" ' O Lord, open Thou our lips,' said Compton, ' and our mouth shall show forth Thy praise.' "

II.

" By the way, you were speaking about Macready as we drove along," said Toole presently.

" I called on him at Cheltenham. It had been said that he was not over-polite to some of the profession, and in a general way that he was ex-clusive and difficult of approach. I found him the opposite of all this ; a fine, distinguished old man, white hair, very courteous, and with a most pleasant smile, a trifle melancholy perhaps—a touch of Werner, but a gentle and human touch.   We had a long chat ; he spoke of his last appearance, and

MR. MACREADY.

I said how I honoured him for making it his last when he said it was, the more so that I knew he had had many tremendous offers to induce him to reappear.   And, of course, this was very honourable in Macready, seeing that he had managed Drury Lane often at a loss, in the interests of art, and only retired just in time to keep a remnant of his fortune to live upon in a quiet way. Considering that he was not rich, there was something very dignified in refusing offers of great and certain sums to appear again, especially in the face of examples of ladies and gentlemen, operatic and otherwise, taking not one farewell but half a dozen. He talked about his children, and referred to his not allowing them to go to the theatre, and said, by the advice of Charles Dickens and John Forster, he was glad that he had at last been induced to let his children see him act. As to his last appearance, he said he did not believe in an actor remaining on the stage after his powers were at an end ; he thought a man should retire in the zenith of his strength ; and he believed he had played ' Macbeth ' on that last night as well as ever he had played it. I confirmed this ; and it pleased him very much when I told him that I had stood at the entrance of Drury Lane on his farewell appearance for five hours, with his great admirer and friend, Lowne, whose collection of Macreadiana, by the way, is the finest of the kind I have ever seen. I have played more than one joke off upon Lowne in that direction. Once we were at Shrewsbury together. He found there a remarkable old portrait which he wanted for his Macreadiana. The price was too much, he thought. He was going to call again about it the next day. In the meantime I called, bought it, arranged with the dealer to tell Lowne a wonderful story about a collector from London, and a large sum voluntarily paid for the picture. The dealer must have done his part very well ; for at night, after the play, Lowne was rather down in the mouth. The subject of the Rugeley poisoning case was very rife at the time. Palmer had begun his awful work in the very hotel where we were staying. I encouraged Lowne and Loveday to talk about it. We parted finally for the night in a rather creepy condition. When Lowne put his light out I was outside his door. Suddenly I heard an alarmed exclamation, followed by a hasty striking of matches, a sigh of relief, and then the words, ' Ah, the dear fellow ! This is kind !' He had found in his bed an ugly parcel (I had had the picture impressively wrapped up) containing the rare portrait supposed to have been carried off by a London rival."

III.

Lowne himself tells a story of Toole which business men will appreciate. When Toole was in America, Lowne acted as his treasurer on this side of the Atlantic.

" The last amount he had to receive in New

York was eleven hundred pounds. He forwarded it to me in a bill payable at sight, drawn by Duncan Sherman and Co., on their London agents. I received it in the middle of a mail of my own," said Lowne, telling me the story when he had shown me his Macreadiana. " I was excessively busy at the time, and put it into a drawer, thinking I would pay it into the bank the next day. I went on with my work, but presently found myself remarking, ' Business is business : pay that cheque in this afternoon.' I took a cab and paid it to Toole's credit.

" Two days afterwards I heard that the American firm had failed. I had not seen the announcement in the morning paper, but soon verified the—to me—alarming fact. I rushed off to the bank.

" ' Is the eleven hundred I paid in recently placed to Mr. Toole's credit ?'

" They referred to their books.

" ' Yes,' they said ; ' it is.'

" ' Thank you very much,' I said, greatly relieved, I need not tell you.

" I telegraphed to Toole at Kingstown : ' Don't worry ; the eleven hundred draft is all right.'

" ' What is the matter with Lowne ?' was Toole's remark to Loveday, showing the telegram. ' What does he mean ?'

" The news of the failure had not reached them.

They soon knew what I meant when they landed in Liverpool.

"There's another curious circumstance about that draft. When Tóole paid the money at New York the clerk said, 'Will you have the draft at thirty days or at sight?'

"'Well, I don't know,' said Toole. 'It will make no difference to me whether it is at thirty days or at sight.'

"'Ah, well, perhaps you'd better have it at sight,' said the clerk; and Toole is under the impression to this day that the clerk knew what was going to happen, and was anxious to serve the English comedian. Actors, I need not say, often inspire very kindly feelings in the breasts of people with whom they are unacquainted. I know it was so particularly in the case of Macready.'

IV.

"THE Macreadiana," which has been mentioned as the finest collection of the kind my host had seen, is indeed unique so far as Macready is concerned, though it is probably outrivalled by Mr. Irving's Edmund Kean collection (arranged by Mr. Lowne), and there are other kindred works, no doubt, on a still more elaborate scale. Mr. Lowne's " Macreadiana " was carefully consulted by Sir Frederick Pollock when he was editing his most complete " Life of Macready."

I spent a day quite recently with the collector, who took great delight in showing me the work, and directing my attention to its chief points of interest.   He began to work on these memorial volumes in the year 1847, when as a youngster of nineteen he had imbibed a strong admiration for the great actor.   The first contribution to it is in the shape of an autograph from Macready himself, who sent the following words, " *Toujours de la poésie, c'est ne pas vivre ! on n'existe qu'en prose,* William Charles Macready, June 17th, 1847." From that time his book has grown, till now, incorporated with Sir F. Pollock's memoir, it has reached five folio volumes of some 500 to 600 pages each.   " It begins," writes Mr. Lowne, " with the account of the opening of the Birmingham Theatre by the elder Macready, in 1795, and many of the bills of that theatre and of old Covent Garden are here, with that gentleman's name as an actor of small parts.   Macready (W. C.) starts with the *Birmingham Gazette* of 1810, containing the account of ' a young gentleman named Macready,' having made his *début* the previous evening as ' Romeo,' the notice at this early age (he was then but seventeen) foreshadowing his future greatness.   This paper was sent to me by a gentleman of Birmingham, whom I never knew, but who wrote me with it a charming letter, by the kind offices of dear Henry Irving, my good friend for many years. Macready is traced through his early provincial career by many rare playbills, wherein we find him playing in all sorts of dramas—the *Wood Dæmon*, for instance, in which he represented 'Hardyknute'—'Charles II.' in *The Royal Oak*—'Belcour' in *West Indian*—'Puff' in *The Critic*. The father became bankrupt in 1809. Here are the MS. copy of his address to the Birmingham audience when giving up the theatre, and later the list of bankrupts in which he appears as William Macready, dealer, 12th November, 1809. All the bills of Macready's first nights in London are here with the notices of his performances, and the playbills extend throughout his London career down to the final night at Drury Lane in 1851. Especially noticeable are bills of his management, both at Covent Garden and Drury Lane, which are all but complete as far as first nights of important plays and revivals are concerned. In one of his country engagements, the manager announced Shakspere's play of *The Stranger !* I wonder what Macready said when he saw this bill. All the great actors of this period, and many of those antecedent to it, are represented both by portraits and autograph letters.   There are letters of Garrick, one a remarkably fine one to Dodsley, to whom Davy administers a sharp rebuke on his querulous and quarrelsome conduct regarding some now-forgotten drama of his.   Another shows Garrick's care in the preparation of his correspondence, being a rough draft of a letter to Edmund Burke, declining to act a drama which had been submitted to him on account of his ' duty to the public.'   There are letters of Siddons, the Kembles, both John and Charles, Macklin, Edmund Kean, King, the Jordan, Bannister, Munden, Elliston, and all the earlier stars who acted with Macready, and the modern drama is represented in a like manner. There is the autograph agreement which Phelps signed and exchanged with Macready when the latter went down to Southampton to see and engage him, as described in Pollock's book, and also Phelps' previous letter to B. Webster, agreeing to an engagement at 10*l.* per week : there are letters of all his later contemporaries, both male and female—Helen Faucit, Charlotte Cushman, Fanny Kemble, Mrs. Nisbett, Mrs. Warner, &c., &c. Among the autographs I may mention one of Charles Kean, who writes to Moran of the *Globe* ' For God's sake, take care of us to-night.   The *Morning Herald*, formerly kind to me, has changed its colour—milk turned to gall, entered

one of the Macready masonic clique, &c., &c.'
The authors are represented by letters of Browning (referring to the publication of his ' Strafford '),
Knowles, Talfourd, Bulwer, Dickens (one of the
most prized of these is the letter written by the
great novelist to Macready, the day after he left the
stage, and which was very kindly given to me by my
friend Jonathan Macready), Thackeray, Jerrold,
Forster, and others. There is a delightful letter of
Jenny Lind to Macready, shortly after his return
from America, and referring to the famous Astor
House riots in 1849. The portraits are very
numerous, and all his contemporaries are illustrated;
there is in addition the entire series of Lane's
admirable portraits of the actors and actresses of
Macready's period, and George Scharf's etchings
illustrative of his management at Covent Garden.
Newspaper cuttings run through the whole book,
including those which show Macready after his
retirement from the stage, subsiding into the
quiet teacher of village boys in a school of his
own promotion, with occasional appearances as a
Public Lecturer or Reader, for the benefit of such
Institutions as the Bristol Athenæum and such
like. The volumes close with the published
records of his death and funeral, and later with
the reviews of Pollock's book, accounts of the
correspondence, including Macready's own letters,

upwards of a hundred, of which not the least interesting to me as the collector are those written to myself before, and subsequent to, his retirement from the stage.   The latter show the ' trembling hand,' and some of the very latest are simply signed by him, the substance being written by the kind and gentle lady who happily still lives and bears his honoured name.   Fifty years subsequent to his first London appearance, viz. on September 16th, 1866, he wrote me a beautiful letter in reply to one of mine congratulating him on the anniversary, to which he touchingly refers.   It is attached to the playbill of his first night.   There are here, also, the playbill of the night of the Astor Place riot, sent to me from America by a dear friend, and the pamphlets relating to the Forest riot sent me from Philadelphia by the late Mr. Gemmill, the manager there, and all the papers relating to the Bunn v. Macready row in 1836, with the trial, and a curious print of the fight."

V.

" MEMORANDA :—To ask J. L. T. about G. V. Brooke and Miss Kelly," I read from my notebook, upon which hint my host recalled the incidents I desired to chronicle.

"The last time I saw G. V. Brooke," he said,

" is one of my pathetic memories. It was on the eve of his departure for Australia in the ill-fated *London*. He and I went to visit T. C. King in Queen's Square, Dublin.

" Everybody thought King was dying, and he certainly looked as if he had not long to live. We

MR. G. V. BROOKE.

went into his bedroom, and I was very much impressed with the sorrowful manner in which they greeted each other, their deep rich voices adding to the solemnity of the occasion. Poor Brooke was very much moved at the close.

" 'Well, my dear Tom,' he said, 'please God, you'll soon get better.'

" ' God bless you, Gus,' was King's reply, ' you are very kind; but we shall never meet again.'

" Brooke leaned over the bed and kissed King very tenderly on the forehead, and said 'Good-bye!'

" We had a cab at the door. When we got into it Brooke said, ' Poor Tom! I fear he is right; we shall never see the dear fellow again.'

" Brooke sailed a few days afterwards for Australia, and was drowned at sea. King is still living.

" I played with Brooke only on one occasion. It was in Liverpool, for his benefit. *The Pretty Horsebreaker* was put up for me, and *The Wife* for Brooke. He was an excellent actor, impressive, strong, romantic, and a kindly fellow. Nothing could have been more manly, not to say heroic, than his death.

" Miss Kelly.—I went to see her with Irving (she was ninety), at Feltham. An old-fashioned cottage harpsichord and other accessories. You might have thought you were in an atmosphere of a hundred years ago. She was the original, you know, in *The Maid and the Magpie;* famous as the robber's wife. Acted with Edmund Kean and Macready. Spoke in high terms of Grimaldi.

She gave me the buckles which Bannister used as 'Master Walter' in *Babes in the Wood*.

"We went twice to see her. She was one of the Babes. She greatly admired Irving. Would have him stand in the light where she could see him.

MISS KELLY.

"She was a very interesting old lady. She built the Royalty, you know, which was called Kelly's Theatre—the first time in London an actor or an actress had given his or her name to a theatre. She lost a great deal of money one way and another in the management—seventeen thousand pounds. She was famous as a teacher.

Miss Keeley was one of her pupils.   She brought out pupils.

"Mr. Gladstone was going to put her on the Literary Fund in recognition of the benefits she had conferred upon the dramatic art, &c.   Irving and myself used our influence in this direction, but she would not accept it.   She was very anxious we should try and get the recognition; that was all she wanted.   She was rather proud of what she had done, and said all she desired was the smallest public acknowledgment that she had been of some service.

"When we left—it was not very long before she died, poor thing—I remember she stood upon the stairs saying good-bye to us; and taking Irving's hand and looking at me, she said—not in a maudlin or morbid way—that life was uncertain. 'If I go first'—looking reverently upwards—'I shall keep places for you two.'"

VI.

A BRIGHT, breezy drive back to Whitby, an hour's rest, then two hours of acting, a frugal supper (the convalescent's *régime*, with gout on the watch for its victim's thoughtless moments), and I had other unsatisfied memoranda in my note-book that were the cues to further Reminiscences.

"If there is any pet story," I said, "which you

desire to keep for your own particular telling, now is your time to reserve it. When these papers are printed and published, the best of your anecdotes will become chestnuts, to quote the Americanism referred to in our opening chapter."

"And serve them right," he said, "at least I shall not be misrepresented. Our Anglo-American scribe has been at his annexations very much of late. And won't he go it when the book is announced. I would not mind so much if he did not try and disguise his hand by mutilating the incidents in which I am concerned."

"Don't mind him," I said, "he will blush and amend his ways when he reads these chronicles ; and if he does not, we shall have a circulation of millions to his hundreds."

I remember saying to General Horace Porter in New York, when I asked him to let me tell his story about ducks in " Irving's Impressions," that if he consented he would for ever afterwards lose it as an oratorical adornment of his excellent speeches. Further, I explained that he would be plundered of his witty anecdote by hundreds of other story-tellers, who would quote neither him nor me. At a royal reception a year or two later, the Grosvenor Gallery echoed to the laughter of the Prince of Wales and a number of literary guests " over one of the best stories they ever heard." It was the duck story recited by a popular American, who in his sparkling narrative, forgot both Horace and Joseph. All writers and all story-tellers have this kind of experience. Being a modest man, and liking to see other people happy, I have often listened with feigned amusement to several anecdotes which, if not my own invention, had at least made their first appearances in print with my assistance. A curious experience of Mark Twain's in this direction I have narrated somewhere. It was during an evening at Bateman's, when the genial colonel lived at Kensington Gore. Mark Twain had told several good stories. Irving had also contributed to the "anecdotiana" of the evening. One of his stories was so good, that I suggested to Clemens (Mark Twain) he should make a note of it as an example of English humour. He did so with a grave smile. The next day I repeated the story to another American friend, who sent me one of Twain's latest books containing the anecdote in question. Mark Twain, I believe, credited me with being a wag, and he must have enjoyed the subtle humour of Irving. But Mark is a professional humorist. He would invent the kind of fun in which I had unconsciously indulged. But this is by the way. Mr. Toole has some further reminiscences of the " Dodger."

VII.

"I HAVE had several jokes with the 'Dodger's' clothes," says, my pleasant host. "Years ago, in Dublin, it was a common thing for purchasers of old clothes to haunt the neighbourhood of the Post Office in Sackville Street. When you were posting your letters you would be addressed as 'Captain' or 'Colonel,' as the case might be, by one of these merchants, who would tell you his business, and press you urgently as an army man to let him relieve you of your cast-off garments. There was one old gentleman in particular who accosted me on several occasions. At last I invited him to come to me at Brunswick Street and I would show him what I had in his way.

"'I feel quite sure it won't be worth your while,' I said, 'but since you are so pressing I will have the articles got out for you.'

"'It's my business, Colonel. I shall have the greatest pleasure in calling, and I'll give ye the best price, as I always do.'

"I had the Dodger coat put up in one little parcel, the waistcoat in another, and the trousers in another. I numbered them 1, 2, and 3, and arranged with the servant that she was to bring them down as I called for them.

"My friend from the neighbourhood of the Post Office arrived in due course. I received him with a continuation of my previous fears that I had nothing which was worth his while; but, I said, at the same time I would show him two or three little things that might be regarded as cast-off.

" ' Sorr, it's myself that should apologize if any is needed. I'm very glad, sorr, to call upon you, and give you my best attention.'

" I called to the servant. She brought No. 1. It was rather carefully tied up. The dealer talked and chatted while he undid the knots.

" I said it was a pleasant day. He said indeed it was. I said Dublin was a fine city. He said I might say that. I complimented Phœnix Park. He agreed with me that it was a lovely park ; and as he did so he unfolded the Dodger's coat. I pretended not to notice that the parcel was undone.

" You know what a coat it is. The tails reach down to the ground. The original coat had to be lengthened. It is a most extraordinary-looking garment, very dilapidated and worthless in appearance.

" I saw him lift it up to the light, look at it, turn it over, and presently exclaim, ' By St. Patrick ! and what the divil's this ? What do you do with a thing like that, sorr ?'

" ' Well, I wear it occasionally.'

" ' Oh, sorr, it must 'a bin a long time ago

before ye wore a thing like that. Well! . . .
Well!! . . . Well!!!'

"'Ah,' I said, 'I was afraid it was no good
your coming.   Better not trouble; better not
show you the other.'

"'Oh, yes,' he said, 'since I'm here better see
it, sorr—if it's something more marketable.'

"Whereupon he opened No. 2, the Dodger's
trousers.

"'Great Heaven's!' he said.   'Upon my soul,
I never saw such a thing in all my life! . . . Have
you nothing more in this way?'

"Yes, I said, there was another little parcel, a
waistcoat; but I was afraid it would be no good.
In fact, I regretted that he had taken the trouble
to come.

"'Oh, no trouble at all, sorr.'   He no longer
called me colonel; he would not even honour me
with the title of captain.   'No trouble at all, sorr.
Very glad to wait upon gentlemen in the way of
my business.'

"The waistcoat was a settler.   He held it up to
the light; he laid it down upon the trousers.

"'Well, upon my soul, sorr, what ought I to
say to such things as these? They're not worth
a copper for pieces. What in the world d'ye do
with such apparel?'

"'Oh, I wear it,' I said.

"'You wear *them?*' pointing to the clothes.

"'Yes.'

"'Where, may I take the liberty of asking?'

"'Oh, sometimes at a masked ball,' I said.

"'Oh, my darlint, that's it, is it? Well, now I can fit ye; I can fit ye with the smartest soldier's coat ye ivver saw.'

"He had an eye to business, you see; but he did not fit me with the coat, and of course for giving him all this trouble, which afforded me a good deal of amusement, I endowed him with an annuity, paid quarterly; and I conferred a similar token of my appreciation and sympathy upon a boy who took part in a little comedy some years afterwards at Belfast."

"Mr. M'Gee was a swell tailor there, and is, I believe, to this day. He had a fine business, and conducted it in a fine manner. Sothern used to patronize him.

"One of his customers, an old friend of mine, introduced him to me : and we arranged that at about the time when we should be chatting with him—half-past two in the day—a boy from the hotel should wait upon him with a parcel containing the Dodger's coat and trousers. He was carefully instructed by the boots at the hotel to give that parcel into no other hands except those of Mr. M'Gee; to inform him that the Mayor had sent him, and wished Mr. M'Gee to put the clothes in order for him in time for the grand ball which was the event of the following night.

"I had been introduced to the famous tailor, and we were just beginning a pleasant conversation about the material of a beautiful vest that would be the very thing for me; 'a most elegant and lovely piece of velvet as ever came from a loom,' he assured me, 'the height of the fashion,' a thing he could entirely recommend. He was a fine, handsome, showy-looking gentleman, rather pompous, but very agreeable, and had a fine, rich, and varied vocabulary. He was interrupted by one of his assistants informing him that a messenger from the Mayor wished to see him.

"'Oh, indeed. You'll excuse me, gentlemen, a moment. I won't detain ye a moment. It's a messenger from the Mayor—most important, gentlemen—a highly-cultivated and altogether a very fine representative of civic power. Excuse me a moment, gentlemen.'

"We excused him; continued to examine the vest-pieces, but followed him with our eyes, listened to him with our ears.

"The boy stood there with the parcel in his arms. Mr. M'Gee approached him.

"'What is it, my boy?'

"'It's from the Mayor, sorr. I was to give it

into no other hands but yours, sorr. It's some clothes which the Mayor wishes you to put in order for him for the grand ball to-morrow.'

" ' Very well ; give the parcel to me, my boy, and tell the Mayor I will attend to it. First, let's see what it is.'

" His assistant took the string from the parcel, and Mr. M'Gee stepped back with an exclamation.

" ' What the divil's this ? What d'ye mean ? Who sent ye with these things ? '

" ' The Mayor, sorr.'

" ' Oh, the Mayor sent ye, did he ? Come here —come here, my boy.'

" The boy followed him a little distance into the shop, and then Mr. M'Gee gave him a whack that echoed through the place.

" ' Ye young blackguard ! Take that to the Mayor, and take your dirty garments to the Mayor,' and he threw them at the boy, who howled tremendously.

" This was a little more than we had bargained for. The pride of Mr. M'Gee was evidently awfully outraged, and the outrage had aroused an evidently violent temper. We got the boy quietly out of the place with a comfortable solatium, and rescued the clothes, which seemed to be in imminent danger of destruction.

" It took us a considerable time to explain the joke to Mr. M'Gee, who by-and-by professed to enter into it and to be considerably amused. I gave him an order for that elegant fashionable vest, but I don't think he ever quite got over the liberty we had taken with him. Sothern, who afterwards mentioned it to him, told me, indeed, that M'Gee would never forgive me. It was not simply that he objected to be made ridiculous, but it hurt his pride that a stranger to him and an artist belonging to a profession he admired should treat him with disrespect."

VIII.

THE description of Mr. Lowne's great collection of Macready illustrations suggests to Mr. Percy Fitzgerald that I would like to chronicle a collection which has been formed, " relating to our great living actor, Mr. Henry Irving." Mr. Fitzgerald tells me he began this pleasant task many years ago, " by first getting together all that I could conveniently find, and without extending my researches (as Mr. Lowne has done) to matters only indirectly connected with the central figure, such as illustrations of contemporary performers, &c."

Having secured all that belonged to the actor's

past, it was not difficult to keep the collection "up to date."   The result is nine huge folios, forming an extraordinary mass of pictures, reports, criticisms, and playbills, all "laid down," as it is called, and mounted, and all referring to one conspicuous personage of our time.   Dr. Burney, the musician, amused himself by collecting in this fashion all that had been printed or engraved of his great friend, Garrick; and the number of portraits, in character and otherwise, thus brought together is very remarkable.   " But, in this respect, it can hardly compare with what has been done in the case of Irving, whose refined features are better known to the public than any one of his time, and have been reproduced again and again. In this respect, he may be said, in the racing phrase, to have 'beaten all preceding records.' It would be an interesting inquiry to discover what is the foundation of this *pictorial popularity*, as it may be called.   It might be traced to the having a sympathetic nature, and this is no doubt the secret of the charm exercised by such persons as Mr. Gladstone, Cardinal Manning, and Irving. Irving has been portrayed in every form known to the limner, from the official, elaborately-finished portrait by Millais and Long, down to the little rudely-engraved woodcut in the corner of a penny paper."

In Mr. Fitzgerald's collection there are some thousands of these " counterfeit presentments "— fine photogravures, lithographs, wood engravings, caricatures without number, innumerable scenes from plays, many of these very effective and clever —" in short, the picturesque nature and movements of the man appear to be always prompting and inspiring the artist."   In their arrangement Mr. Fitzgerald has taken care to collect pictures that illustrate each play—the various scenes, with the sketches of the chief actor—the bills and the criticisms from all the journals : from the hurried two columns, written off hastily at midnight after the performance, to the more thoughtful and scientific essay in a monthly review.   " When the *Corsican Brothers* was brought out, an elegant and artistic *brochure* was issued, containing views of the scenes in delicate colouring, which it might be difficult to procure now.   There are numbers, too, of large and spirited portraits—big heads with ' immaterial legs ' as Elia hath it, and in gaudy colouring, but spirited withal, which one would not know where to seek for to-day.   Even the advertising agents and dealers have utilized him, and Messrs. Allen, of Belfast, have issued certain designs for wall-posters, which are admirable. Some enterprising Italian warehousemen have employed this firm to prepare a ' Mephisto-

pheles,' which is strikingly excellent for the likeness, and well coloured too.   There was a time
when our actor was one of the best caricatured of
men—a homage, it may be said, which, like that
paid by vice to virtue, is the tribute offered by
disappointment to success.   Now he is so secure
in the public favour, and so *rangé*, that we rarely
see a caricature.   The most successful of these
picadores is Mr. Alfred Bryan, who knows
every nerve and muscle of his Irving by heart,
and must have done some thousand images of
him in his day.   These, it must be said, are bold
and vigorous, though exaggerated, and one must
admire the firm stroke and brilliant touches.
Nor has the etcher been idle.   There are two
pretty idealizations of the *Vicar of Wakefield*, and
of *Faust*, which are worth securing, and two published long ago by Mrs. Noseda of the Strand.

"During the run of *Hamlet* and *Eugene Aram*,
there appeared some fine crayon drawings which
were photographed and published, but which are
now unprocurable.   In proof of the quickening inspiration exercised by this great actor, it may be
added that during the run of *Faust*, a clever
young lady used to dash off spirited sketches
of 'Mephisto' in red water-colours, and these
were sold in the shops at five shillings a piece.
The attitudes were varied according to the

suggestion of the moment, and the likeness excellent. Nor must we forget the pleasing *Faust* souvenir, which originally appeared in the *Art Journal*, and of which a vast number of copies were sold. There have been also little statuettes modelled of him in this character. Indeed, the sculptor has been no less busy than the men of brush and pencil. Mr. Onslow Ford's full-length " Hamlet " is well known, and is a fine specimen of the *bravura ;* but it is rather heavy in treatment, and would have been more effective in bronze. There is a bust of him by Jackson, done many years ago for Mr. Bateman, rather formal and magisterial in expression. There are but few photographs ' in character '—for the ' Merchant of Venice ' was, I believe, one of the last occasions on which Irving consented to sit, or stand. There are some good ones, however, of him as ' Dr. Primrose '; but none as ' Hamlet,' ' Richard,' ' Benedick,' ' Mephisto,' or ' Romeo.'

" Passing now to the literary portion of the collection, we shall find an astonishing aggregate of details. There are some half a dozen " lives "— and sundry controversial pamphlets, including ' The Fashionable Tragedian,' some of attack, some of defence, panegyrics, assaults, burlesques, &c. There are the two volumes of ' Impressions of America,' and criticisms from every journal, many from the provinces. Very curious is the record of the American tours with the American criticisms. These were furnished to me regularly by the unfailing thoughtfulness of the manager of the company, and are fairly complete. The Irving visit produced a flood of literature, and the leading criticisms were collected and published, while Mr. William Winter, the most distinguished of the Transatlantic critics, has issued his own in a pretty volume. The American bills are interesting, and illustrative of the country, were it only for the pennyworth of dramatic bread that accompanies the intolerable quantity of advertisement. 'Irving bills,' as the dealers have it, are almost impossible to procure, and some of those early ones, in which his name figures modestly as a lord or courtier, bring high prices. I have a few relating to the old Surrey and St. James's days. A set of the Lyceum bills would be but a *lean* one, and scarcely reach beyond two score; for as each play has 'run' about a year and more, each night's bill is, of course, a repetition of the preceding one. Then there are great numbers of letters, invitation cards, bills of fare, for the path of our actor is marked by profuse hospitalities.

"Such, then, is this curious and, as I may call it, flattering memorial. I need hardly add that our friend himself takes a great interest in its progress, and supplies occasionally something of interest. One is inclined to speculate, what will be the final limit of the undertaking ? To what extent will it expand ? I must confess, that at this moment it has gone beyond measurable or even manageable dimensions. I can contemplate it as the years roll on, like Mr. Weller's Shepherd, ' a swellin' wisibly,' encroaching on the next shelf, one huge armful added to another, as the *Times* develops in a club library. Inconvenient as this prospect may be, I shall welcome it cheerfully, as it will be a sure sign of the lengthy life and happy prosperity of the amiable and brilliant person whose career is thus recorded."

VI.

MISCELLANEOUS NOTES, ANECDOTES, AND SPEECHES.

Keeping up appearances—A local hit—"Still I am not happy"—Creswick and the song—Paying her rent—Halifax and Huddersfield—The Kirbys—Shepherd and the bandit—Sheridan Knowles—The Trebizonde magician in trouble—Lord Dudley and the performing dogs—Morality and the stage—Toole and his serious friend—An Edinburgh speech—Cant and slander rebuked—Other notable speeches.

I.

DURING a few pleasant days at Harrogate we cleared up a budget of miscellaneous notes. The little theatre was crowded every night. An interesting feature of the audience was a number of Catholic priests from an adjacent religious establishment. The reverend gentlemen enjoyed the plays immensely. They were particularly delighted with *The Serious Family*. Toole had many callers at the hotel. We drove to Knaresborough one day, and devoted the rest of our time to the Reminiscences, with the following results. It was originally my intention to write something about

Harrogate, but I find it best to keep in view the end and aim of my sojourn there. Do you remember the old story of the Scotchman who had the reputation of never turning aside from the work he had in hand ? A London visitor to the village where Sandy was a servitor made a bet he would break the charm of Sandy's firmness of purpose. The Scotchman went to the well every morning for water. The Londoner scattered half-pennies along the road. Sandy looked down curiously at the first ; paused on seeing the second ; at the third put down his pitcher. The Londoner and a native were in hiding, but looking on. The native trembled for his bet ; the Londoner chuckled ; but just as Sandy was about to pick up the Londoner's pence he raised his pitcher and walked on his way, remarking, " Nay, when I coom oot to get bawbees, I'll get bawbees ; when I coom oot to get watter, I'll get watter." That is how the chronicler of these Reminiscences feels. When he goes out to describe Harrogate, he'll describe Harrogate ; when he goes out to chronicle Toole's Reminiscences, he will not turn aside for all the tempting bits of local character and colour Harrogate can provide.

II.

" On one of my first seasons at the Theatre Royal,

Dublin, I played *Uncle Dick's Darling*. It was capitally put upon the stage, and everything went well until the last change after the dream. There's ' a scene rise and sink.' The top went up ; the other portion would not move. I was obliged to step over the portion that wouldn't sink. The boys in the gallery hissed.

"At the close, when they called me, I went forward and said that a little mishap had occurred, ' but you ought not to blame us. We were only two or three minutes trying to sink that bit of scenery, and you have been two or three weeks trying to raise a ship in Kingstown Harbour.'

" The hit took wonderfully. It went with roars of laughter and applause. A ship had sunk in Kingstown Harbour, and there had been a good deal of hostile criticism in the press in regard to the futile efforts which had been made to raise it.

" After *Aladdin the Second* in Dublin, in which my catch phrase, ' Still I am not happy,' was very popular with the boys, I went for a little trip to Killarney ; and on my return spent an evening at the Italian Opera. I was ' observed,' as the tragedians say. A boy in the gallery called out, ' There's Toole in a private box, and still he is not happy !' Then other boys called upon me for a song. I dissembled ; but finally had to retire."

III.

"The ballad in *Uncle Dick's Darling* was written by our old friend Wrighton—his friends used to call him Billy Wrighton—who was not only a delightful composer of simple ballads, but used to sing them in a very charming, sympathetic, old-fashioned way. I made him a present of a silver jug as a souvenir of the ballad, the words of which were written by Clement Scott. The publishers, in order, as they said, to make the song popular and sell it, insisted upon putting my name upon the frontispiece as if I were the author. I expostulated, pointing out to them that even if I could write a song, a sentimental one would not be exactly in my line. However, they were business-men, and they arranged the matter in such a way that on the title-page it did appear as though I was more or less the author of the ballad, and at a party at Wrexham, where I sung it one evening, the company took such an interest in the alleged composer that I could stand it no longer, and declared publicly that I was not the composer of that pretty ballad, and could not, under any circumstances, go through life as an impostor. The publishers were very indignant at this, but I couldn't help it. Besides, as I told them, if I permitted this kind of thing to go on, they might be asking me to write an opera, or setting me forth to the world as a rival of Verdi or Balfe."

IV.

"When I was playing *Uncle Dick's Darling* at Birmingham some years ago," begins my genial host, in response to sundry questions of the chronicler, " in the rush for gallery seats a man broke his leg, and his chief distress was not that he had broken his leg, but that the accident had happened in the gallery.

" ' I have never,' he said, ' been in the gallery before.   The pit was so crowded, I couldn't get a seat.   I am a commercial traveller, and I shouldn't like my firm to know that I was in the gallery. It would lower me in their estimation.'

" I need not say that Mr. Rodgers, to whom this confession was made, never alluded to the particular part of the house in which the poor gentleman came to grief.   I believe, out of pure sympathy for him, Rodgers was willing to have hinted, if necessary, that the painful event had occurred in the dress circle.   What a thing keeping up appearances is!   I suppose the poor chap was right.   He knew his firm."

V.

" One day, during an engagement which I was fulfilling at Bolton, Loveday and myself were sitting in our room at the Swan Hotel, he making up his accounts, I writing letters, when a woman walked in, banged down some money upon the table and said, ' There's the rent ! '

" George looked at me : I looked at George.

" ' Oh,' I said, ' that's the rent, is it ? '

" ' Yes,' she said ; ' and we must have some repairs done.'

" I said, ' Certainly.   What do you want doing ? '

" She said she wanted the rooms papered and whitewashed.

" ' Certainly,' I said, ' they shall be papered and whitewashed.   Anything else ? '

" ' The windows don't fit properly.'

" ' They shall be made to fit,' I said.

" ' Thank you.'

" ' Anything else ? '

" No ; she didn't think there was.

" ' Well, if you think of anything else you have only to mention it and you shall have it done.'

" ' Will you give me a receipt ? '

" I turned to George and said, ' Give the lady a receipt.'

" George smiled ; looked bewildered ; gave her an order for a box, putting it in an envelope ; bowed ; gave it to her, and she left the room.

" Of course we followed to listen. There were others at the bottom of the staircase, and we saw the situation at once. Opposite to us was a room, out of which a man came. We looked in and saw there was a sort of rent audit going on—the collection of rents for some local estate.

" We heard our visitor explaining how kind we had been, and we half regretted we had not told her she should pay no rent at all in future. But presently there was an altercation between her and an official, who said they had agreed to do nothing of the kind, neither in the way of white-washing nor papering : whereupon she grew con-siderably excited ; and more particularly when the official, having been up to the audit-room, came back and said she had not paid her rent at all.

" In the meantime, of course, we had put matters right, and after our unexpected fun, George re-warded the old lady, and we interposed with the agent on her behalf and secured her the envied whitewashing and papering we had promised."

VI.

" There is supposed to be a good deal of jeal-ousy between Halifax and Huddersfield, just as there is between St. Louis and Chicago, and other rival towns in America. Knowing this, when

I went into a shop at Halifax to purchase a very showy handkerchief to use in *Uncle Dick's Darling*, I said, in a casual way, that I thought of going to a funeral in Halifax, and was told this was the kind of handkerchief they used. The shopwoman said, 'Indeed, sir, then it's new to me; nobody in Halifax would think of wearing such a flaring affair for a funeral, or anything in a serious way.'

"'Well, I don't know,' I said; 'they told me in Huddersfield you do queer things in Halifax. And that's where I got my information.'

"'Oh, Huddersfield,' she said, 'they tell awful lies at Huddersfield. I assure you it is nothing of the kind. Huddersfield—it's like Huddersfield, that is! A fine town, Huddersfield. Dear me! dear me! what lies they will tell at Huddersfield!'

"She was very angry; and I thanked her for putting me right."

VII.

"Some years ago I was arrested for income-tax. It was at Edinburgh. I went down to give some readings and recitals. The amount was six pounds. I had already paid it in London. Of course, I hadn't my receipt with me. The man said he was very sorry to arrest me, and I encouraged the tragedy for a little while, pretending I would allow him to carry me off, and all that sort of thing; but finally I paid the money under protest, with an additional fee of ten shillings, which I have never received back from her Majesty's Commissioners, though I made more than one application for it.   Fancy running the risk of being taken to gaol by the Government when you've paid the money!   It shows how little they know sometimes about these things in official quarters.   They used to follow actors about in this way all over the country, and many an artist has had to pay twice over, as I had.   But they arrange these things better now-a-days—don't know how, but they do."

VIII.

" When Creswick, the tragedian, came to Edinburgh during one of my stock engagements there, *Black-eyed Susan* was put up.   As a rule Wyndham played ' William,' but it had become traditional that the tragedian should add this character to his *rôle*.   Creswick therefore claimed ' William ' and played it.

" I was very popular, and explained to Creswick that after ' William's ' yarn about San Domingo Billy, I was accustomed to sing a song.   Wyndham, when he played the leading part, had not objected to the song, and on this occasion he was especially reconciled to the innovation.

" Creswick, with the solemn geniality of the tragic actor, agreed to the new business, ' Very well, then, Mr. Toole, after the passage relating to San Domingo Billy, I will call upon you to sing a song.'

" Poor Creswick ! He did so. The boys encored it. I sung another ; they encored that, Creswick, as the hero, ' William,' having to stand all the time. I felt a little wicked over it, and offered him a seat, which he took.

" I think I had five encores ; and I believe that is the only time I can charge myself with not having shown full and complete respect to the serious hero of any piece in which I have been engaged. Creswick accepted my apologies, and I don't think the incident changed our friendship."

IX.

" DURING one of my starring engagements in Dublin, Miss Louise Keeley was a member of my company, and travelled with myself and wife. Her father and mother, the late Robert Keeley and the present Mrs. Keeley, came over on a visit. They had a box one night at the theatre, and I played two of Keeley's celebrated pieces. The first was called *The Governor's Wife*, in which Mrs. Keeley used to be very successful as a funny little cockney woman. Keeley was ' The Governor.' On this occasion I played Keeley's part; Louise played her mother's. We were both rather shy and nervous with two such really clever predecessors looking on. *Ben Bolt* was the other piece ; one of those wild, mad, melodramatic plays by T. B. Johnstone, in which I was a low comedy sailor who did wonders against the villain of the piece. One of my great scenes introduced some business with a red-hot poker. It was all very curious and unnatural, but was accepted in a serio-comic spirit by the audience.

" Keeley was very complimentary about the evening's performances, and after supper took quite an artistic interest in giving me suggestions, telling me what he did with the poker, taking one out of the fender and giving me a lesson, as if the matter was really serious. He was a very earnest little chap, had a naturally odd and comic look, bald-headed, very small, a grave humorous face, and a serious way of delivering very comic lines.

" ' They gave you a tidy poker,' he said. ' I'll tell you what I should do to-morrow night. I used to do it. Have the poker very red, and when you confront them, blow upon it and say : " I'm keeping it warm for you." '

" He took the poker from the fender and showed me this odd bit of business, as I said before, with the greatest earnestness.

" For one of our Dramatic Fund's benefits, I acted with the Kendals in *Married Life*. The Prince of Wales was in a box. I played 'Coddle ;' Buckstone played ' Dove.' Somebody sent round a suggestion from the Prince that I should give an imitation of Buckstone if ' Buckie ' didn't object. " Buckstone did *not* object. 'Not at all,' said he, when I mentioned it. ' I shall be glad to hear you do it.' " In the next scene, where we met, I ventured to oblige my friends. The imitation went immensely. Buckstone, laughing as heartily as the rest, said, ' He didn't know what I was doing, but I affected a peculiar tone of voice which seemed very odd to him.' "

" Shepherd was a character at the Surrey. Shepherd and Creswick had the theatre together, you know ; and they each had their seasons, too. Creswick, when he was in authority, always played Shakspere and the high-class legitimate, and Shepherd played melodrama and strong domestic pieces. Fernandez, who since those days has made a distinguished mark in the profession, was cast for a very small part by Shepherd, and com-

plained of it, resisted playing it. Shepherd said,
' Why it's a far better part than many in Creswick's
répertoire—more gig and go in it. I don't see

MR. FERNANDEZ.

how you can complain; you've got the limelight
on you during the whole of the last act !'

"One day, when I was talking to Shepherd,
the super-master came to see him, and after some
preliminary business said he wanted some advancement; he had been playing in the company nine

or ten months, had done his best, and would like to get a speaking part with a little increase of salary.

"'Who are you?' said Shepherd. 'Let me see. What do you do in the piece we are playing?'

"'Well,' said the super-master, 'I'm on in that scene with the brigands. There are five of us sitting round the table. You are playing cards with us. I win fifty louis-d'or of you every night.'

"'Very well,' said Shepherd; 'all right. I'll advance you certainly. From to-night you shall win one hundred louis-d'or.'"

X.

"I DID not know Sheridan Knowles. He was before my time; but when he became what is considered serious, and used to preach, I heard him hold forth at Islington, and did not think much of it; but he was a very able man, no doubt, a fine dramatist, and a singularly droll fellow. Planché told me a capital story of him. I believe it is in his book of reminiscences; but that does not matter, does it? No. Well, this was the story. There was an actor at Drury Lane named Binge, who played kings and princes, both in the regular as well as the lyric drama. On the occasion in question he was a young count, who loved a gipsy girl, but deserted her for a great lady, and in the second act there was a sort of gala-day celebration of the betrothal of the count to the fine lady ; but there was something in the story which rather

"A 'NORRIBLE TALE !"

went to suggest that, after all, the gipsy was not altogether out of the running. Well, Knowles had been in front until nearly the end of the act, but had to go away, and he was anxious, or professed to be so, to know how the piece ended ; so he went behind, and getting as near to Binge as he could at the wings, without, of course, being seen by the audience, he called to him in a loud whisper, 'Binge!' The actor looked over his shoulder, and in an aside asked, 'What is it?' 'Tell me,' replied Knowles, 'do you marry the poor gipsy, after all?' 'Yes,' answered Binge, a good deal worried at the question, and making signs with his hand behind his back for Knowles to stand further away. 'God bless you,' said Knowles, seizing the warning hand, you were always a good fellow!'

"I was playing the 'Gravedigger' at the Queen's in Dublin with T. C. King. At the moment where I sing 'A pick and axe,' &c., the gallery boys called out 'A 'Norrible Tale!' and would not let me go on, demanding 'A 'Norrible Tale.' The manager was Harry Webb. It was a freak of the gallery boys to try and get him out. He made a speech on this occasion while I was standing in the grave, informing the house that this was Shakspere, not farce, and that neither Mr. Toole nor himself would desecrate the Bard by introducing comic songs; at the close of which the gallery shouted, 'Go to bed, Webb; go to bed!'"

XI.

"While I was at the Gaiety, I engaged for a series of performances at the Standard. It had been arranged that I should have a vacation.

But suddenly Hollingshead came to me and said I must play in *The Princess of Trebizonde*, a first-rate part having been written for me. You know Hollingshead's emphatic way. He went to the Douglasses and tried to get me off the Standard engagement, but they held on to me. Hollingshead was not to be baulked. He arranged to play *The Princess* late enough to allow me to fill both engagements; so I played *Uncle Dick's Darling* at the Standard, and the magician in *The Princess* afterwards at the Gaiety. I had to dress in my brougham, change my 'Uncle Dick' clothes, and dress as the 'Trebizonde Conjuror' as I drove from the Standard. The moment I arrived at the Gaiety the overture for the burlesque was played, and I was on at the rise of the curtain. One night in Finsbury Square my brougham was upset, and I was turned out partly dressed in my 'Trebizonde' robes. Fortunately they were ample, and I pulled my kind of decorated gaberdine around me and surveyed the situation. Almost immediately a crowd of men and boys were similarly engaged.

"'A conjuror off to the Raglan,' said one.

"'No he ain't, he's agoin' to do a turn here. Now then, guvner, where's your bit of carpet? Where's your daggers and your spinning dishes, and your magic cabinets?'

"'Yas,' exclaimed a third, 'tip us a sample o'

yer style, ole chap, we'll put your oss on 'is legs. Come on, ere y' are.'

" 'And here *you* are if you'll get me a cab,' I said, showing them half-a-crown ; and I can't tell you how glad I was when I got to the Gaiety and was told I was only three minutes late."

XII.

" I WAS playing a short engagement with my friend, James Rodgers, at the Prince of Wales's Theatre, Birmingham, when I received a letter from Lord Dudley asking what would be my terms to give my entertainment and bring my poodle dogs with me for a children's party at Witley Court.

" My first impression of the letter induced me to think it was a ' sell,' possibly the work of Sothern or some other practical joker ; but my manager knew Lord Dudley's writing, and pronounced the application perfectly genuine, though evidently made under some misapprehension. I wrote to his lordship, informing him that he had made some mistake ; that I never gave entertainments, either with or without dogs, at private parties ; my place was the stage, the only platform upon which I thought an actor should perform in the way of his profession.

" I received in reply a very polite note, explaining how the error had arisen, which I understood and appreciated at once. The fact was I had been present at a little party given by Mr. Gilbert Farquhar, at the house of his mother (Lady Farquhar), in Berkeley Street. Mr. Hollingshead, Mr. Arthur Sketchley, Mr. Arthur Cecil, Mr. Archibald Wortley, and others, having lunched at Berkeley Street, were informed by her ladyship that she was going to give a children's party on a certain afternoon, at which we all promised *con amore* to be present and help to amuse the little ones. It was a very pretty sight, and a very interesting occasion. The children of the Prince and Princess of Wales and Lord and Lady Dudley were there, and many others. We did conjuring tricks for them ; we played the trial scene from ' Pickwick ; ' I was ' Serjeant Buzfuz,' Sketchley was ' Mrs. Cluppins,' George Grossmith played ' Winkle,' and Archie Wortley was ' Sam Weller ;' I sung ' He always came home to tea,' the song I was then singing in a burlesque at the Gaiety. The children and Lady Farquhar were very delighted, thanked us profusely ; and, after we had finished, a performer with some trained poodle dogs, who had been engaged and paid for by Hollingshead, was introduced to wind up the entertainment.

" The children, Lord Dudley was good enough to inform me, had gone home telling their parents how pleased they were with Mr. Toole and the

dogs, and Lord Dudley had very naturally mixed
the poodles and the comedian up together. Hence
my correspondence with Witley Court."

XIII.

" WE have often discussed the Puritanical
view of the stage," I said, "and I have a
memorandum of yours not to forget the Edinburgh letter."

" Yes, I know," said Toole ; " a very amusing
incident, and instructive, too, I think you will say.
While I was acting at Edinburgh, some years ago
—I was starring at the time—I received a letter,
very well written, but a very canting letter, ad-
vising me to withdraw from the stage and lead a
proper life : a man of my intelligence and ability
ought to do something better.

" I did not answer the letter, but called on the
writer on Sunday afternoon.

" He had a very handsome house in the suburbs.
All the blinds were down.

" I rang the bell : sent in my name. There
seemed a little commotion in the hall. I was
shown into a room.

" Presently a solemn-looking gentleman in black
entered. He spoke with rather a Scotch accent.

" 'Glad to see you, Mr. Toole,' he said.

" 'Thank you,' I said. 'I thought it best to

call on you—better than writing. I am anxious to know what you propose to do for my wife and family.'

"'What I propose to do?'

"'Yes. You wish me to leave the stage. It is my living. I thought you might have some idea of an annuity.'

"'An annuity? Eh! dear me! I had no idea of the sort.'

"'Then what do you mean?'

"'I was not thinking so much of you, Mr. Toole. It's the other people in the company.'

"'My dear man,' I said, 'it's very likely they are very much better than I am. I may be quite a libertine, for all I know, compared with others; but we played *Dot* yesterday, and I am quite sure that a piece of that kind is calculated to make quite as good an impression upon an audience as any sermon that you or your minister could deliver. It is full of humanity, and carries a striking and touching lesson.'

"'Eh, mon! I like you very much, Mr. Toole, and I'm sure you're quite right. I laughed awfu' at ye when I saw you play the "Dodger."'

"'Then what do you mean?'

"'Eh, mon, it's the wife that's serious.'

"'Oh. And that's the reason why all the blinds are down, is it?'

"'The blinds are down,' he said, 'because it's the Sawbath, ye ken.'

"'And do you think, then,' I asked, 'you are serving God by shutting out the beautiful fields and flowers that He has given you?'

"'Aweel, I never thocht of it in that licht,' evidently gradually getting very much ashamed of himself.

"Finally he would insist upon introducing me to his wife, who invited me to tea. She was very severe and starchy at first, but we got on pleasantly at tea-time, and they have since invited me on several occasions to visit them."[1]

XIV.

THIS question of morality and the stage was referred to in a speech which Mr. Toole made at

[1] A correspondent, hearing that I am "writing about Mr. Toole," sends me the following:—"About 1866 or 1867, a lady visiting a well-known photographic establishment in Regent Street, where the portraits of most of the talent and beauty of the profession may be found, upon some of the latest productions being brought to her notice, made some disparaging remarks concerning actors and actresses, and generally expressed a very poor opinion of them, their calling, mode of life, habits and associations. A clergyman present, overhearing her, quietly observed, 'Well, madam, I do not take your view of it. Both Mr. Toole and Mr. Bedford are my parishioners, and they attend my church regularly; and two better parishioners I do not wish for, both for attendance and for their support in every charitable work that is brought before them.'"

the Theatre Royal, Edinburgh, in 1883, on the last night of an engagement there, under the management of Messrs. Howard and Wyndham. He had appeared during the evening in *Your Life's in Danger*, *The Upper Crust*, and *The Spitalfields Weaver*. At the fall of the curtain he was called again and again, and, finally, a speech being loudly demanded, Mr. Toole said :—

" Ladies and Gentlemen,—As I am announced in the programme this evening to say a few words to my friends, I will commence at once. But I am in my usual state. I never know what these few words are to be, for, I assure you, it is a most difficult task to find words strong enough to thank you for the very hearty and genial reception accorded to me during this visit. I have often said that it is to me a great labour of love to play before my Edinburgh friends, and when friend Howard says to me, ' How many pieces will you play in to-night ? ' I reply, ' As many as you please ; ' for as long as my Edinburgh friends do not get tired of me, I assure you I do not get tired of acting to them. (Applause.) I have to thank also my friend Howard, with whom I have been ·associated for many years—I taught him to play ' Rob Roy '—(laughter)—for the admirable manner in which the pieces have been produced, and the genial way in which he always receives me. Like Mr. Doublechick, I do not like apologies, and I won't apologize for not making a better speech; but I told my Glasgow friends a little story, and I do not see why you should not have the benefit of it. (Laughter.) Some years ago I dropped into a Music Hall in Portsmouth, just to study a little character. The admission was 2*d.*, and the reserved seats 3*d.* (Laughter.) I am happy to say my circumstances were such that I was able to take a reserved seat. (Laughter.) Well, there was a gentleman there who always wound up the entertainment by singing that exciting song, 'The Wolf.' (Laughter.) He had been singing it for twenty years; but that night he had evidently been partaking of something stronger than ginger beer, and when Mr. Jones was called upon to favour the company with 'The Wolf,' he began it something in this fashion. (Mr. Toole here, amid much laughter, sang in a husky voice the first line of the song, 'When the wolf he nightly prowls.') The audience had been a kindly and indulgent one, but his style was more than they could stand, and some hissing was heard. The performer tried it again (Mr. Toole again mimicking him) with the same result. Then the performer, pulling himself together, said : 'Ladies and gentlemen, I am not surprised at your indignation. The fact is I have sung this wolf hundreds of times, and I have sung all the air off him.' (Great laughter.) Well, I must tell you I had to-day a letter from an old friend of yours and mine, Mr. Henry Irving—(applause)—who expressed regret at not being able to appear this year in Edinburgh.   He is hard at work in preparing for his great revival of *Much Ado about Nothing*.   He said in his letter, ' Make a nice speech to my Edinburgh friends for me,'—but of course I could not lay claim to do that, I am too modest—(laughter), ' and say it would afford me great delight to appear before them previous to going on my American trip next year.'   There are two or three reasons why I regret the absence of Irving, who has done so much for the stage, because there is a matter which ' does make me so wild '—(laughter)—on which he could have spoken so well.   I read a letter the other day in the *Scotsman*, which, as an actor, I think one is bound to protest against. (Applause.)   It was written evidently by one of the Chadband School, and it counselled young men to avoid the theatre, where vice and immorality were made to appear fascinating and attractive.   I am sure you will agree that it is a piece of impertinence for any one at this time of day. to write such a letter—(applause)—especially in a city like Edinburgh, where Sir Walter Scott lived, who was a great lover and frequenter of the theatre.   (Applause.) The theatre is now supported by the highest and best in the land.   It was not long since I, with a little company, had the great honour and pleasure of being received as guests by the highest lady and gentleman in the land—the Prince and Princess of Wales—and of playing before them at their Sandringham home. (Applause.) And it is a pleasure to think that so many gentlemen connected with the church now attend the theatre. I am sure few of them would countenance such remarks as those to which I refer. They are a relic of a bygone age. (Applause.) I shall leave them, ladies and gentleman, to the writer's conscience; I shall not discuss here the private character of an eminent actress whom the writer mentions—an actress whom I had never the pleasure to meet in private—on whom he made some horrible remarks. I have sent a copy of the *Scotsman* with that gentleman's letter in it to her husband—(loud applause)—who doubtless will treat the traducer of his wife as he deserves. (Applause.) I feel bound as an actor, who has met with so much kindness on the Edinburgh stage, to protest against any one making such uncharitable remarks. (Applause.) But I will not detain you further, for the hour is late and I have still some classic ballads—(laughter)—to bring before you. I have been spending a little time with my friend Sims Reeves—(laughter)—and you will hear how my singing has vastly improved. (Laughter.) My friend Howard, indeed, intends to bring me out in Italian opera—(laughter)—on my next visit to Edinburgh. And when you are in London, if you drop into Toole's Theatre, I am sure you will get a right hearty welcome." (Cheers.)

Mr. Toole is one of the most successful of public speakers. Whatever the occasion he is invariably equal to it. A collection of his post-prandial utterances would fill a volume. I am tempted to give a few additional instances in illustration of his pleasant faculty of oratorical chat. In July, 1875, when Mr. Henry Irving presided over the Thirtieth Anniversary of the Royal General Theatrical Fund, at Freemason's Tavern, Mr. Toole, in proposing "The Health of the Lord Mayor," said it had been customary to suppose they could not have too much of a good thing, but he saw so many good actors who could have proposed this toast so much better than himself, that he felt some diffidence in undertaking the duty. Having recently returned from the United States, he need scarcely say he was "interviewed," and that he had the honour of being received by the President, who, amongst other things, asked him if he was not an Irishman. He asked, in reply, if the President had ever heard of St. Mary Axe, because he was born there—in the Lord Mayor's ward.

(Laughter.) Whether this was told to the gentlemen of the Press or not he did not know. The Lord Mayor had referred to " Richard the Third," a part which might soon be played by his friend Mr. Irving, who, he hoped, would not interfere with the classic performances at the Gaiety Theatre, where he (Mr. Toole) was at present engaged. Lately there had been a great noise, as he thought, behind the scenes, but on inquiring into the cause, he was told it was " two Scotch gentlemen fighting over the way." [2] (Laughter.) Since then he had closed the windows. (Laughter.) He felt this hospitable reception, as they all did, a great compliment, and he hoped when the Lord Mayor came to the theatre they might be able to entertain him. He could only say that, among other achievements, the Lord Mayor, whose health he now proposed, had won all their hearts.

Three years later Mr. Toole presided over the Anniversary Dinner of the Royal Theatrical Fund. The story of the " Tiny Tim " who ate the goose (which appears on page 65) is, as previously stated, a reminiscence of the Chairman's speech on that occasion, the leading points of which it will be interesting to reprint. In giving the toast of the evening, Mr. Toole said :—" Gentlemen,—Three

[2] Mr. Toole's dressing-room at the Gaiety overlooked the front of the Lyceum Theatre.

years ago, when my dear friend and old professional comrade, Henry Irving, had the heavy responsibility I have now to discharge, of proposing from this chair the toast of the evening, he related how twenty years before, a boy, he had stood at the door of the London Tavern, eagerly watching the guests as they assembled for this Fund's dinner, delighted when he recognized the face of some popular actor or celebrated man. That boy was Irving himself, who has continued his hero-worship until he too has become famous. (Applause.) I, gentlemen, have to ask your forbearance and sympathy for another boy, a different kind of boy. My boy attended the first Festival of the Royal General Theatrical Fund three-and-thirty years ago, also held at the London Tavern, when the late Mr. Charles Dickens presided, holding every one spell-bound by his graceful allusions and charming humour—except that the commonplace boy I am introducing to you, who, in spite of his admiration for acting and his early reverence for Mr. Charles Dickens, was too busy cramming himself with jellies and creams behind a screen to be spell-bound. (Laughter.) He was the son of a well-known City Toastmaster, who was often taken by his father to banquets to sit in the gallery with the ladies, or to be slyly fed by the waiter in some secure hiding-place within convenient distance of the sweets.   That same boy has, in the way of business, eaten a good deal of pasteboard food of a less toothsome character since then, for the benefit of a great variety of theatrical funds, and is now rather bewildered at his own boldness in presuming to occupy this chair—a position which he has seen filled by so many distinguished men ; and in having to appeal to you seriously on behalf of the Profession we have met to serve.   It is not for a boy with this early training—a jelly-boy in fact ; ahem ! no connection with Dickens's Mrs. Jellyboy, and Boola Boola Gha—to attempt to take you over the ground which has been so skilfully, so eloquently, and so pathetically travelled by the illustrious men who have preceded him ; but this boy wishes to touch your pockets through your hearts, and induce you to give large sub- scriptions to a most admirable Fund, a Fund which preserves self-respect by enabling the actor to help himself, and to make some provision against the day of disaster and misfortune.   (Applause.) Dropping third person metaphors, perhaps you found out who my boy was as soon as I mentioned him, for as I left my cab this evening I heard a voice from a little crowd at the door say, " That's Toole ! " and another voice reply, " In coorse it is, stoopid ; everybody knows Toole ; " so as disguise is impossible, I will in my own name tell you of an experience of a stage supper which the name of Mr. Charles Dickens recalls to me, and which is not without its bearing on the business before us."   (Applause.)

[Here the speaker told the story of the child-actress who, as " Tiny Tim," developed an extra-ordinary appetite.]

" Not a bad illustration this, gentlemen, of the kindly spirit we so often find behind the scenes— the spirit of helpfulness and unaffected generosity —which, I am bound to say, distinguishes the dramatic profession, and to which I hope to appeal with success this evening.   Most actors could quote by the score similar examples of unselfish-ness in the young—and you know actors never do grow old.   The late Mr. Paul Bedford called with me on Mr. T. P. Cooke, at his house in Torrington Square, with the view of enlisting his services in aid of a charitable benefit then being organized; and, in the course of conversation, Mrs. Cooke and another old lady being present, we touched on the drama of *One Tree Hill*, when T. P. Cooke (Tippy Cooke) said, ' Very ·unfortunate, would be glad to oblige, but there was no part *I* could play in it—only one sailor—and he was an *old* man, which made it quite out of the question for me, of course.' Considering Mr. Cooke was at that time well on in the seventies, I may be excused for doubting if successful actors can grow old—(laughter and applause) ;—but it is for the unsuccessful I plead to-night ; for those who have lost their powers, or have retired, from ill-health or advancing years, without sufficient resources ; and I ask you not to think, because I have not attempted to be pathetic that there is no pathos in the subject, or any want of serious, earnest purpose in my aim. The merits and benefits of this most admirable association have been dwelt upon and extolled in past years by his Royal Highness the Prince of Wales, and such men as Mr. Charles Dickens, Mr. Thackeray, Mr. Phelps, Mr. Buckstone, Mr. Irving, and last year by that warm friend of the drama and its professors, his Grace the Duke of Beaufort. I cannot hope to approach their eloquence, or their power of bringing gracefully before an assemblage such as this, the claims it is the duty of a Chairman to advocate ; but, speaking as an actor, on behalf of actors and respecting actors, I will say that for economy of management, for plain fulfilment of the purpose for which it was designed, for freedom from jobbery, and I may say from snobbery—for bringing relief and cheerful succour for those worsted in the battle of life, for an honest endeavour to inculcate manly independence throughout the ranks of a profession, this Royal

General Theatrical Fund is second to no institution in the country.   I would appeal earnestly to all young actors and actresses to join it.   I pledge my word to *them*, that they will never regret the small annual sum it may cost them ; and I pledge my word to *you*, gentlemen, that whatever you think fit to subscribe this evening will be properly and faithfully applied.   I leave purposely to our indefatigable treasurer, and most excellent man of business, Mr. John Hollingshead, the duties of explaining to you the statistics of the fund ; and I would like to tell you—as he will be too modest to do so—how splendidly he has worked since he has been treasurer, and how through his untiring exertions the Fund has been enormously benefited.   Before sitting down, I am reminded of a circumstance that occurred to a celebrated comedian, the late Mr. Harley.   In the early part of his professional career, and before he came to London, he took a long journey in a coach through Buxton—I don't mean our old friend, but Buxton in Derbyshire—before railways were known ; and he had as a fellow-traveller an elderly gentleman who became greatly interested in the vivacity and entertaining powers of Harley, who delighted him with a fund of anecdote.   At the end of the journey the old gentleman shook hands with Harley, heartily thanked him for his pleasant companionship, and said he had never enjoyed travelling so much. Well, as they say in drama, ' time rolled on ; ' Harley never saw his fellow-traveller again, but during his first London engagement at the English Opera House, now the Lyceum, he learned that the old gentleman had died, bequeathing Harley a handsome town house well furnished, with a cellar fully stocked with admirably selected wines. Now, gentlemen, I assure you I have, ever since I heard this story, now many years ago, tried hard to make myself agreeable to all elderly gentlemen—(laughter)—I meet in my travels, but nothing has yet come of it, and I am prepared to discount my chances this evening —nay, this moment. If there be present any, I will not say elderly, because I've shown that the glamour of things theatrical prevents *our* growing old, but any gentleman, of any age, who has derived the faintest scintilla of amusement from anything he has heard to-night, I implore him not to remember me in his testamentary dispositions, but to gladden my heart far more than that would do, by giving now, this evening, while he is alive—I think I may say all alive—as largely as his means allow, to the fund on whose behalf I most earnestly appeal. (Cheers.) Following the example of the great people at Berlin, we are now holding our Congress, and I am Plenipotentiary for the

Royal General Theatrical Fund.   Gentlemen, it
is only by your liberal aid and generous co-
operation that our Congress can insure peace and
tranquillity of mind to the unhappy, help to the
unfortunate, and solace to the bereaved.   Gentlemen, it is in your power to achieve these noble
ends, and to make me very happy as well.   For
let this Theatrical Congress of 1878 be quoted
hereafter as having fulfilled its mission handsomely and effectually, and I shall look back upon
my presidency with as deep a satisfaction as
Prince Bismarck ; for you will have made me feel
that, inadequate as my best personal efforts have
been, your indulgence has overlooked my short-
comings as a Chairman and a speaker, while the
claims, the merits, and the usefulness of this
Theatrical Fund have, like our great countryman,
Lord Beaconsfield, driven their points home, and
have spoken to your hearts and feelings the best
kind of English with vigour and success.   Gentlemen, I now leave in your hands, with the fullest
confidence, the toast of the evening, ‘ Prosperity
to the Royal General Theatrical Fund.’ ”   (Loud
cheers.)

Responding to the toast of “ The Visitors ” at a
recent banquet of the Scottish Water Colour Society
at Glasgow :—“ Gentlemen,—Later on in the evening, in the character of ‘ Paul Pry,’ I have to make
a remark to the assembly, ‘ I hope I don’t intrude ;’

and you will permit me, on behalf of the guests, to remark, we hope we don't intrude. But I am sure we do not after the very handsome banquet you have given us. I don't know how all of you will end this happy festival, but I know I shall finish by going to the theatre to-night. (Laughter.) It is for me a great delight, and I feel sure to all of us, to spend this charming afternoon here. (Hear, hear.) It is my good fortune and privilege to be the personal friend of a great number of artists in England, Ireland, and Scotland; amongst them Sir Frederick Leighton, president of the Royal Academy; the president of the Royal Scottish Academy, and indeed of all the good fellows connected with the art, and I may say I never enjoy myself better than when I am in the company of painters, because they are the tenderest, the gentlest of men. I spend most of my leisure time in going to the Royal Academy, and the Grosvenor. I was kept away from the Grosvenor Gallery once, though, from the fact that my portrait was hanging in that gallery, and being a modest man I was rather shy about it. (Laughter.) There was one day that I was looking at it, and two old ladies were looking at it too. One old lady said to the other, 'Who is that?' 'My dear, I do not know,' said the other old lady. 'It is the portrait of a gentleman.' That was complimentary to me at any rate.

(Laughter.) 'He looks very serious,' said one of the old ladies again ; ' I think he is a clergyman.' (Laughter.) ' Or a scientific lecturer,' said the other—(renewed laughter)—and then, looking at the catalogue, she added, ' It is the portrait of a Mr. Toole.' The other said, ' I don't know him, but I fancy he is an actor.' (Laughter.) ' Poor fellow,' was the other's reply, ' he is a tragedian, he looks so sad.' (Mr. Toole said this with such characteristic humour that loud and prolonged laughter followed.) I must thank you very much for the very charming way in which you have treated us as guests. It is a great privilege to be here. Three years ago I happened to be in Glasgow when this delightful gathering was held, and in attempting to make a speech I remember I said that if you invited me again I should try to make a better. It has been rather worse. (Laughter.) But if you invite me next time I shall try to do better. (Renewed laughter.) You know Mr. Alma Tadema. I will tell you a little story about Mr. Tadema. He is full of fun, like me, you know. He and my friend Colin Hunter are nearly always laying traps for me in the way of chaff. ' I should like, Tadema,' I said to him, ' your advice about a picture. A friend of mine wants to get a picture into a gallery.' Mr. Tadema went on to expatiate about the different galleries. Perhaps I should

try to get it into the Royal Academy, and the
Grosvenor Gallery is very good. Then he
asked what the picture was like, and I produced

MRS. KENDAL.

the picture. It was a small, unpretentious thing,
a common little drawing of myself in character—
(laughter)—fourpence a thousand, you know.
(Renewed laughter.) Now, just a word of advice
to the artists. I happened once to be lecturing

on painting, and I made the remark that the best
thing an artist could do to improve his taste was
to clean his *palate*. (Laughter.) But I won't
detain you any longer. I hope we shall all
behave ourselves so well that you will invite us
another time. (Laughter and applause.)

At Liverpool and Manchester, at the latter
end of 1887, Mr. Toole followed Mr. and Mrs.
Kendal. They had followed Mr. Irving and
Miss Kate Terry. The Kendals are deservedly
popular in the North, but on this occasion Liverpool had not been as lavish as formerly in its
patronage of their entertainments. Mrs. Kendal made a speech on the occasion in which she
seemed to upbraid Manchester for its infidelity to
the house of Kendal. Her husband stood by her
side while she spoke this memorable address.[2]

2 "It is many years since Liverpool playgoers have had so
rich a choice of dramatic art as they have had during the past
week, when at one of our leading theatres Mr. Irving and his
company have appeared in the *chef-d'œuvre* of the many famous
Lyceum productions, while at the other Mr. and Mrs. Kendal
have presented a series of high-class dramas, exquisite alike in
instruction and in representation. . . . Notwithstanding the
extraordinary counter-attraction in Liverpool, the Kendals at
the Court Theatre have been drawing exceedingly good houses,
and their performances have been received, as usual, with great
cordiality. At the close of the play of *The Ironmaster* on
Saturday evening, Mrs. Kendal appeared before the curtain
in company with Mr. Kendal, and delivered the following

Some short time previously Mr. Wilson Barrett had spoken of his boyish ambition "five-and-twenty years ago," when he had stood as a boy outside the Princess's Theatre in Oxford Street, vowing to himself that one day he would play "Hamlet" in that very house; Mrs. Kendal had also distinctly announced her intention to retire from the stage when she reached the age of forty.

brief address, which was received with loud applause:—
'My good friends, we have again been in Liverpool, and have met with the same encouragement that we have always previously experienced here. It is true that we have on this occasion met with some very strong opposition by the great production of *Faust* at another theatre. For the first time we have seen tiny vacant spaces before us, and I have noticed some white antimacassars, which I abominate, *entre nous*. Still I shall come here again. I thought at first that you might probably have been frightened in consequence of the rubbish which appeared in the papers the other day about fires in theatres. Now I may say that I have been every night on the stage for I do not like to say how many years. I have been surrounded by numerous jets of gas, and a great deal of lime-light has been thrown on us both. But we have never met with any accident. So that when you read in the papers of these alarms about the danger of fire, don't believe them. I assure you that you will be just as safe in a theatre as in the street, for in both places we must trust in Providence for our lives.' (Applause.) It will be observed that Mrs. Kendal in her kindly desire to reassure theatre audiences as to the safety of theatres from fire, altogether omitted all reference to the far more fatal cause of loss of life, that of panic. However, everybody will give the genial actress credit for good intentions in departing from the customary rule."—*Liverpool Daily Post*, October 10th, 1887.

It is necessary to mention these incidents for the non-actor reader to understand the following speech which Mr. Toole made at the close of his Manchester season. During the interval between *A Mint of Money* and *Paw Claudian*, Mr. Toole stepped to the front of the curtain and delivered three of his well-known addresses upon "Chemistry," "Astronomy," and "China," all, of course, amusing. He then addressed his audience as follows :—" It would be difficult for me to convey to you in a few words how grateful I am for your constant kindness to me on each occasion of my visits to this city. This has been one of the most pleasant visits I have ever paid to Manchester. It is very difficult to know what to talk about. It is so much the custom in Manchester for ladies to make speeches—(laughter)—that I feel rather nervous. (Renewed laughter.) Of course had my wife been travelling with me—(laughter)—I might have been able to persuade her to do it—(laughter)—but if any lady would like to step down here and say a few words I should be very glad. (Laughter.) I suppose it is no good telling you, ladies and gentlemen, that I am going to save up money and retire when I am forty years of age, because I have just turned that point—(laughter)—and I do not think of retiring for a good many years. (Loud applause.)

I love my profession too much for that, and I am too proud of your applause and of the friends I have made in Manchester. (Applause.) A friend of mine said to me the other day, 'What about your popularity? Why don't you get the horses taken out of your carriage somewhere?' Well, in the first place I do not keep a carriage, and I never saw the horses in it. (Laughter.) In the next a gentleman in France, when he was told, 'Just now you had your horses taken out of your carriage,' replied, 'Yes, and I have never seen them since.' (Laughter.) Well, then, I will tell you a little story. I might begin: 'About twenty-five years ago'—(hear, hear, and laughter.) Oh, I see you know all about that. (Laughter.) Well, then, I must thank Captain Bainbridge earnestly for the very admirable way in which he has produced my pieces and for his kindness and courtesy to me. There is no theatre in which I play with greater pleasure, or which has more pleasant associations. I must also thank the gentlemen of the press. A friend of mine said to me, 'You never get cut up in Manchester.' I replied, 'I do not know about that. I often appear in three pieces.' (Laughter.) I have seen great changes since I first appeared in Manchester, many years ago, but there is one thing that never changes, and that is the warm support,

the hearty greeting, and the welcome which you
always give to me.   I thank you very sincerely,
and I hope the same friendship will always exist
between us."   (Loud applause.)

At the close of *The Butler* season in London,
the acting-manager, being loudly called on to
speak, said :—" Ladies and gentlemen,—I beg
your pardon, but you don't happen to have seen a
great coat about anywhere, do you ?—rather a nice
one, almost new, nice velvet collar, silk lining, and
all that sort of thing, don't you know.   Cannot
think what I have done with the overcoat.   Anything in the pockets ?   I should think there is
something in the pockets ! There are two left-hand
gloves, if they weren't they wouldn't be left ; a
copy of Bacon-Shakspere or Shakspere-Bacon—I
hope somebody will be able to save that somehow.
There is a season ticket for Toole's Theatre—the
number is known and stopped.   There are four
free admissions to the stalls on payment of the
customary fees.   (Laughter.)   There is my latch-
key—how on earth I shall be able to get in to-night
without raising the neighbourhood I don't know.
There is a farcical comedy by an amateur, in eight
acts.   Any one finding it is requested to forward
it without delay to the Inspector of Nuisances.
(Laughter.) Then there are three cough lozenges,
which the finder may keep for his trouble.   There

are six autographs of J. L. Toole, which will be
sold to defray expenses. The eighth part of a
captain's biscuit, which may be sent to the British
Museum; and worst of all, there is *my speech*.
(Roars of laughter.) Any one may have all the
other things if they will only give me back my
speech. I thought of sending a *speechial* constable
after it, but here I am, utterly speechless, though
perhaps you wouldn't think it. The worst of it
is somebody may have stolen my speech; he may
be learning it now, and may deliver it in Trafalgar
Square. (Laughter.) If you should hear anything extra good at any of the theatres during the
next few weeks, you may depend it is quite likely
some actor or dramatist has found my coat.
(Laughter.) I won't detain you any longer, but I
must tell you how glad I am to see you and to come
home again. There are many reasons for coming
home; I felt that many London friends wanted
to see *The Butler*, and had I stayed away much
longer they would have been put to the expense of
going down to Edinburgh, Glasgow, Liverpool,
Manchester, Sheffield, or some other fairy spot, so
I thought I'd come home; besides, I live in
London, and the rent is going on. (Laughter.)
Talking of rent reminds me of a landlord who told
me in Dublin, recently, that when he told one of
his tenants he intended raising his rent he replied,

' I'm glad to hear it, sor, for I've been trying to raise it myself for the last six months, but devil a bit could I do it.'   (Loud laughter.)   I produce a new play by Mr. and Mrs. Merivale at the end of January next, or rather, I should say, when my company have cooled down from the excitement of the Bacon and Shakspere discussion, for upon my calling upon several members of the company at breakfast-time the other morning I found that, instead of studying their parts, they were en-grossed upon Bacon.   Shakspere they always study in the evening.   (Laughter.)   During the Christmas holidays I shall produce Charles Dickens' *Cricket on the Hearth*, for which the box-office is now already open.   (Applause.)   This is a gentle hint.   I won't detain you, but thank you for the warm welcome you have given me to-night.   I know you are all anxious to look for my coat.   Kindly let me know if you find that speech.   I hope we shall have a very merry season.   Come and see me as often as you can.   I wish you good-night.'' (Loud applause.)

Many persons will be inclined to think that the lost coat with the speech in the pocket is an oratorical fiction ; but it is not so.   Mr. Toole had thought out a few words to say and had jotted them down.   He left me at the Ship at Brighton, where, half an hour before his train started for town, he read over the points of his proposed speech. Many of the best impromptu orations of the most eminent speakers are said to be made in this way. But when Toole said good-bye, and hurried off by express to his London work, he carried away some one else's overcoat and left his own behind, and with it, safe in the inner pocket, his extemporaneous speech. When he got to town he wired me, " Have left my coat and speech at the Ship." There was, of course, no time to send them on, not even to telegraph his humorous oration. And this is how it came to pass that " The Butler " made, I believe, a much more laughable address to his audience than the one he had arranged to deliver.

VII.

BEHIND THE SCENES IN KING WILLIAM STREET.

The actor-manager's room—" Making up "—A notable picture —Reminiscences of the Adelphi—The poor man who did not applaud—Dreaming—Toole's admiration for Sims Reeves—The solace of the famous tenor's ballads —At St. Anne's—A lesson for young actors—The stage of yesterday and to-day—London and provincial audiences—French and English actors—M. Coquelin and tragedy—The Bosjesmen and their showman.

I.

No professional room, studio, sanctum, laboratory, or what not, is so interesting to the general reader as the dressing-room of a popular actor. I recall a sketch I wrote years ago of Mr. Irving " making ready to go on " as " Charles the First," which went the rounds of the Press, the foreign Press more particularly, and which crops up every now and then as a new discovery under the scissors of youthful sub-editors. I propose to give " Charles the First " a companion picture in " Caleb Plummer."

On the right of the stall entrance of Toole's

Theatre a private door, screened from view by a heavy portière, leads to the stage-box. If you are permitted to descend the short flight of stairs beyond, turn to the right at the bottom, and at the end of a long and somewhat dingy passage

IN MR. TOOLE'S DRESSING-ROOM.

you will come upon the actor-manager's dressing-room. You will have been preceded thither during Mr. Toole's management by many a distinguished lady and gentleman. H.R.H. the Prince of Wales has been there before you ; so also have the Duke and Duchess of Westminster,

Baroness Burdett-Coutts, Lord Wolseley, Lord Randolph Churchill, Madame Sarah Bernhardt, Mr. Chamberlain, Miss Ellen Terry, Miss Mary Anderson, Mr. Irving, Canon Farrar, and many others well known to fame. The ladies have received as mementoes of their visits one of those little boxes of bonbons which Mr. Toole keeps in a drawer of his desk for his lady visitors, and the gentlemen are not forgotten in the way of such choice or simple refreshment as is considered most acceptable by their naturally thirsty natures.

II.

IT is a notable little room, characteristically decorated with theatrical pictures and photographs of friends and Royal patrons. The door opens in a corner of the room, leaving space behind it for the actor's dressing-table, and for an interesting collection of pictorial treasures which cover every available inch of wall. It is a very simple dressing-table with an ordinary looking-glass, on each side of which there is the usual wire-protected gas-burner. On the table in some confusion are hand-glasses, puff-boxes, chalks, wig-paste, combs and brushes, a small vase of fresh flowers, and if the real work of dressing is going on (which, of course, it is not as a rule when visitors are admitted) you may once in a way see Mr. Fox, the famous wig-maker, in attendance.

"I only employ Fox about once a year, when I play 'Caleb Plummer' or some unusual part," remarked the actor the other night, moving his right eye to emphasize his remarks and call my attention to their impression on Fox, "because as a rule I can get along best alone, much better, I think, artistically; there are little subtleties of colour and other things which one cannot expect Fox to understand."

"Well, I don't know about that," Fox replied. "Mr. —— and Mr. —— wouldn't think of going on any night without I looked in to see that all was right."

"Ah, I daresay," remarked Toole; "but they have not made the art of make-up, and particularly of old men with bald heads, the study I have; my own dresser is first-rate at wigs. And how about Mr. Irving? Why, he invents his own, and his clever little dresser is a perfect artist!"

"And yet we make for Mr. Irving," Fox replied, with a somewhat supercilious smile, which was converted into an anxious one when the call-boy made his last announcement, and the next moment Toole had slipped out of his hands, and, with a wink that was not at all in keeping with the character of "Caleb Plummer," hurried to the stage, and proceeded to enter the honest and virtuous domicile of the Perrybingles, which he did in his own inimitable way, as the living embodiment of Dickens's most lovable creation.

While Mr. Toole as "Caleb" is receiving his parcel of dolls' eyes, and praising the good qualities of "Mr. Tackleton," we will look round his room and make an inventory of his pictures. On the wall, the centre of which is occupied by the dressing-table, is a portrait of H.R.H. the Prince of Wales, in his Scotch bonnet, flanked on either hand by a recent portrait of Henry Irving in private dress, and John Billington as "Lord Hesketh" in *The Upper Crust*. Packed close by are admirable portraits of Mr. Bancroft and Henry J. Byron, the latter a very characteristic drawing in water-colour by Alfred Bryan, depicting Byron as his friends love to remember him, in good health, and good spirits, and with a cigar in his hand as if he had just taken it from his lips to say one of those clever things which are associated with kindly recollections of him, and of happy evenings made happier by his genial presence and sparkling wit. Near the Byron picture is an admirable portrait of Sir Frederick Leighton, President of the Royal

Academy, in a dignified and artistic pose, and matching this photograph on the other side of the wall a likeness of Mr. Routledge, which might have been taken just after his first defeat as a candidate for Parliament, so sad, yet defiant, so conscious of having done his duty, is the expression the camera has fixed upon the sensitive paper. Occupying prominent places among these works are several reminiscences of early Adelphi days, notably a drawing from *The Willow Copse*, representing Paul Bedford and Toole in one of their scenes, Toole being the "Augustus;" and an excellent photograph of Mr. Webster as "Triplet," and Mrs. Stirling as "Peg Woffington" in *Masks and Faces*, "Triplet" with his fiddle, and "Mrs. Triplet" (old Mrs. Stoker) sitting by the table.

On the wall facing the fireplace of this cosy room of the popular comedian, are a series of heads of characters once represented by John Parry (who has a remarkable successor in Mr. Corney Grain), portraits of Grimaldi in private dress and as the clown; Keeley as "Gregory;" Mr. William Black as an admiring friend; Sarah Bernhardt, an admirable study painted upon ivory; a startling caricature of Henry Irving as "King Philip" in his wonderful study from *Queen Mary*; a caricature (by Phil May) of Irving, Bancroft, and

Toole, who are supposed to have been dining out, and are going home merrily; Toole as "Caleb Plummer," sitting by his spotted horse; Paul Bedford and Toole represented in character in

MADAME SARAH BERNHARDT.

the farce of *The Pretty Horsebreaker;* Mary Anderson, a lovely effigy of a lovely woman; young Herbert Reeves, wonderfully like his father —one of Toole's oldest friends; Ward, in Burnand's funny burlesque of *Claudian,* representing the hermit so well played in the original by Willard; Toole on his marble throne as "Wilson Barrett," made up with singular fidelity by the aid of a wax nose, which was a nightly trouble

MISS ELLEN TERRY.

and anxiety all through the long run of *Paw Clawdian;* a copy of the famous picture of Garrick between Comedy and Tragedy; and several groups taken from the current comedies and farces represented by Mr. Toole and his company.

On the right of the fireplace are some classic pictures representing ancient Rome, mementoes of travel, rather incongruously mixed up with a group representing her Majesty the Queen and the Royal family; Liston, as " Paul Pry ;" Sothern, as the " Crushed Tragedian ;" Webster, Mrs. Stirling, Mrs. Stoker and the children in the *Masks and Faces* scenes, where " Peg " visits them for the first time.   In the centre of these is a large water-colour drawing of Toole as the " Artful Dodger," painted in America, and made realistic in the artist's estimation by its surroundings.   The " Dodger " is standing in a street, on one side of which is Drury Lane Theatre and on the other St. Paul's Cathedral.   Over the mantel, upon which a fine mirror reflects the pictures on the other side of the room, are displayed portraits of David James, George Loveday, Sims Reeves, Ellen Terry, Florence, the American comedian ; on the shelf are a few ornaments, and again a vase or two of freshly-cut flowers are to be seen as part of the simple decorations.

III.

I MUST not forget to mention the framed certificate of a vote of thanks from the Yorkshire School for the Blind, in recognition of an entertainment given to the children by Mr. Toole and some members of his company in the spacious lecture-room of that notable institution. A visit to the schools is mentioned in a previous chapter. I don't suppose any artist has ever devoted so much time to the amusement of poor people in hospitals, asylums, and of children in charitable schools as Mr. Toole. A record of these things would fill a volume in itself. He is fond of talking of his experiences on these occasions, the delight of the inmates of convalescent wards gathered together and chuckling in a feeble way at his *Trying a Magistrate;* the less advanced sufferers lying upon their beds to form part of the audience, their pale faces lighted up with smiles. At King's Cross Hospital the patients are carried on their beds to the staircases and landings while Mr. Toole gives his entertainments in the hall, " a touching sight," he says, " which makes it a little difficult sometimes to be funny ; but they are anxious to have a laugh, and often they will applaud quite heartily, forgetting for the moment all their ailments. The other day at one of these affairs I noticed a rather stalwart fellow in his bed. He seemed very pleased with the comic lecture, the Magistrate, and with a funny tale I told them. I noticed him particularly, he had such a cheerful face ; and I did not fail to observe, with not quite so much pleasure as I noticed his pleasant face, that he did not applaud. I went to him afterwards and before I could speak to him he said, ' Thank you, Mr. Toole, I have been so very much pleased ; it is very kind of you,' and then, as if he were about to put forth one of his arms, he said, ' I only wish I could have joined in the applause, but you see I have only one hand, my right arm has been amputated.' It gave me a shock, because I was on the eve, I believe, of asking him, being so pleased, why he did not applaud. The necessity of the encouragement of a little applause to an actor is everything ; if people don't applaud, you are apt to think you are boring them."

The back part of this little room behind the scenes is screened off with a curtain ; if it is partly drawn you get a glimpse of a sideboard, and here the actor exercises the power of summoning spirits from the vasty deep, and not only spirits but wines, not only wines but sweets, and occasionally a dish of sandwiches, and in the season he has been known to conjure therefrom examples of our finest native oysters. In the centre of the room there is a writing-table, frequently full of that curious correspondence which ought to make a very interesting chapter in these Reminiscences ; but you never know until the critic has seen your chapters which are interesting and which are not, any more than you know which are the best scenes in a play until those serious and learned gentlemen have sat in front of the curtain at its first representation and witnessed the performance of the piece.

"Yes," said Toole, one night when he sat in this little room after the theatre was closed, " I like to have my friends about me, if not in the flesh in the pictures. I have often looked round this room in my occasional quiet moments and felt that it is all a dream, and as if I were playing a part all through and shall awaken one day like ' Uncle Dick ' and find myself at that desk in the city. And if I did, what a time I should have had! Poor dear Wright, Keeley and Webster, and Paul Bedford, I think they would belong perhaps to the happiest days of my life. When one is young and getting on, when one is succeeding in the very work one loves and putting a little money by for one's wife and family, that is sure to be a very happy time, is it not? Wouldn't you say so, not only in your private character but as a novelist?"

Toole has a habit of considering me in this double capacity, which accounts for the fact perhaps that he is delighted when I have time to go out with him " character-hunting," as he calls it.

I replied in perfect agreement with him that he had suggested what is no doubt the happiest time in the lives of most men.

" Of course, if I did awaken like Dick I should have escaped some misery and sorrow, such misery and sorrow as I at one time did not think it possible to undergo and live.   After my poor boy died I felt for a long time that life was positively unbearable ; but at last one has to remember one does not live for oneself alone, and one has to remember that others suffer too, that one is not the only person whom Heaven afflicts ; but there, we will not talk of that.   You know what I often do when I feel depressed, going home in a cab ? I have told you before.   It is interesting to recall it at the present moment.   It sounds odd, but we all do curious things, I suppose, if we only cared to confess them.   Of all the music I have ever heard, nothing has ever touched me so much as the singing of Sims Reeves ; I have sat and heard him, and cried many a time, especially at ' Tom Bowling,' the ' Death of Nelson,' and ' Farewell my Trim Built Wherry ;' these songs, as he sung them, represent to me as deep a pathos as the human voice is capable of expressing, and even in the more or less merry songs of that incomparable vocalist, I have always found a touch of melancholy.   I heard you say

MR. SIMS REEVES.

the other day that a wonderful procession you saw on the Grand Canal in Venice affected you so deeply that you felt emotional ; it was so beautiful that it seemed to become pathetic, though it was full of sunshine and gaiety. Well, that is how I feel somehow in regard to Sims Reeves, whether he sings ' My Pretty Jane,' 'Come into the Garden, Maud,' or ' Tom Bowling ;' and often, when I have felt sad, it has been a comfort to me to hum these songs, to hum them pretty loudly, when the rattle of the cab-wheels were especially noisy, and there was no chance of any one hearing me but myself. A charming fellow, Sims Reeves, so modest, has such a wonderful method, and a voice that will never be excelled."

IV.

" DID I ever tell you about my calling on Reeves at St. Anne's, near Blackpool ? Well, I happened to be playing in that enormous hall or theatre by the sea at Blackpool to eight or ten thousand people a day, where Sarah Bernhardt, you remember, on seeing. the audience, was taken suddenly ill, and did not act ; there was a lawsuit about it. I don't wonder at her fright ; the people come into the gardens in their thousands : for certain parts of the hall they have nothing extra to pay to see the performance in the theatre. They are a capital audience; it is impossible for many of them to hear; some of them can, of course; but they see the movement and colour of the stage and all that; some of them have seen the plays before, and recall the incidents in their memory; others are in a theatre for the first time, and find an interest in the performances though they be in dumb-show; and, as I said before, they are most attentive.

"As I heard Sims Reeves was staying at St. Anne's not far away, I thought I would go and see him. I went to the hotel; they said Mr. Sims Reeves had just strolled out; they did not think he had gone far; he had only a few minutes ago finished luncheon. I went upon the beach, he was not there; nor was anybody else, for it was not exactly in the season, and St. Anne's is a quiet, rather unfrequented place. I left the beach and went into the hotel grounds—very pretty and extensive gardens and walks. Under a shady tree, comfortably seated with a newspaper, I saw my friend. He did not see me. I went quietly behind him and gave him a snatch of 'My Pretty Jane,' rendered as lovingly as possible, after his most delicate manner. No response. So I thought I would rouse him up, and I began with an imitation of his *forte* style, ''Twas in Trafalgar Square!'

I had not finished when he turned round, with much amazement expressed upon his features, and—it was not Sims Reeves !

" I felt awfully sold, and I think I blushed ! All I could say was, 'I beg your pardon.' I walked away chagrined, and sought consolation in contemplating the divine loveliness of nature, as our friend So-and-so, the poet, would say.

" Presently I met the same old gentleman to whom I had been singing. He had folded up his newspaper and was walking about. I went up to him. He did not seem inclined to stop. But I said, 'Sir, I fear you would think my conduct very strange just now ; the truth is, I thought you were Sims Reeves,' whereupon he literally rushed away, and when I went into the hotel they told me he thought I was an escaped lunatic.

" He had no sense of humour, you see ; and it is my misfortune sometimes to have too much."

v.

WE drifted from this subject into the art of acting, how it should be studied, the present condition of the stage and kindred topics ; I was desirous of obtaining from him some more comprehensive information in regard to his own methods and views of stage-work than I had hitherto extracted from him. The result was a more than usually sustained expression of opinion, the following note of which is very interesting. Toole tells a story with a careful eye for detail ; but in discussions about his art he is more direct and epigrammatic than elaborate or discursive.

" When I first thought of going on the stage," said Toole, "and long afterwards for that matter, I used to study every kind of acting, watch points of detail, incidents of business, not simply to imitate them but as lessons. There is a lot of talk about teaching acting ; but the only school is the theatre. If a would-be young actor wants to know what acting is, let him go and see the best that is to be seen ; let him see tragedy, comedy, farce, the best of its kind, and let him try and see how effects are made, how certain speeches are spoken, what an actor does in a pathetic speech, what he does in a comic one. He will notice that one man makes his effects one way, one another. When the would-be actor gets home, let him try if he can do anything like what he has seen, or if he can do anything in the way of acting an entire scene of a play by himself; then let him try it on his friends ; if he has any sense he will soon know whether he is a bore or likely to make any-thing of acting. Then, if he fancies himself, let him get into some company where he can play little parts, and study on the stage what he has studied off the stage, and see how things are worked behind the footlights ; if there is anything in him he will get his chance by-and-by.

" Of course, he can't go into the country and join a stock company, as he could have done when I begun my career ; that is a great drawback now, and it works very curiously ; it leads to some young men thinking that if they can dress well and speak well they can act well ; and it is not to be denied that in some cases they have succeeded in persuading managers that they really can. It is a serious thing for the perfection of dramatic art that young men obtain positions on the stage in modern comedy without the training necessary to make them masters of their profession.

" The great test of an actor's proficiency is Shakspere. In the old days nobody ever thought he could do anything if he could not play Shakspere, and I very much question if any man or woman really can interpret the passions, illustrate the joys and pleasures, the fun and frolic and mirth and sorrows of life with real success unless they can speak and act Shakspere. That is why all actors of experience so deeply regret the abolition of stock companies, and why some of them have dreams of a Government subsidy of a National Theatre. Our friend Irving has occasionally put this notion before the public, and more particularly for provincial cities; but it will never be carried out; in spite of the educational advancement of the age, there is almost as much cant against the stage as ever there was. The idea of any minister of the Queen attempting to subsidize theatres would almost lead to a revolution in some districts. Of course, it would be a good thing; it would keep the art intact, it would keep the lamp of dramatic literature burning, and it would hand onwards to posterity the true traditions of great acting.

"Now don't you think I have made something like a speech on acting? I couldn't have done it on my legs, to save my life; if I am very serious for five minutes I feel as if people were saying, 'What is the matter with Toole?' and I think preaching about anything is a bore; perhaps that's because I can't do it; and I am sure my London friends are like that. Now and then when I play some of my serious pieces, I know certain of my London audiences are saying to themselves, 'What is the matter with Johnny?' Not so in the country; not so in Manchester, Liverpool, Glasgow, Birmingham; they like a bit of seriousness, not that their lives are more serious than ours in town, but things don't change so quickly in the great cities outside London as here; life is not so fast, and people seem to go to the theatres

more in the old-fashioned spirit of our fathers—to
be intellectually amused—than is the case in London ; to have their feelings touched, to see the

MONS. COQUELIN.

serious as well as the laughable side of life, and
they seem to have more respect for the great
authors and the great plays ; not that I am com-

plaining—don't think that; I am only referring to matters that strike me in looking back, and at the same time observing the present; and it is pleasant to have a serious chat upon such subjects.

" Now there is one thing which our French friends do, which I am glad to say our English actors don't. Monsieur Coquelin, with all his high-sounding views of art and dignity of the actor, will take a private engagement to appear at an evening party and recite or act in a drawing-room, just as conjurors do, or regular entertainers. When the Comédie Française Company came over here, the members accepted these kind of engagements; even the divine Sarah herself (and a greater actress does not exist) attended receptions as a paid entertainer. It does not seem to me that this is keeping up the dignity of the theatre; it is not the English idea of dignity, any-how. I met M. Coquelin at Aix. He was very talkative and polite, full of inquiries and criticism of Irving, had a lot to say about the principles of acting, and no doubt talked very well—it was good talk, even when it had gone through the sieve of translation; but he seems to forget that he is not a tragedian, neither in his intellectual gifts nor in his appearance. For ' Hamlet' and ' Iago,' for 'Wolsey' and 'Mephistopheles,' an actor wants something in the way of physique very different from the qualities which go to make a low comedian. Coquelin did not seem to realize this, and when he told me he was going to play 'Mathias' and 'Mephistopheles' in London and New York, I laughingly remarked that if he were successful in those parts, I should certainly play 'Hamlet' and 'Macbeth.' I suppose it was not quite polite to say this, but a low comedian is privileged. The truth is, I rather resent the patronizing way in which French actors presume to speak of the English stage. I have seen most of their great players, and I remember Phelps, Charles Mathews, Dillon, Keeley, Robson, Wright, Macready, Anderson, Webster, Buckstone, Compton, Sothern. I look into their past, and want to know where there is a crowd of better actors than these in the annals of the stage ; and, in regard to the present, I recall many incidents of English acting that I don't think were ever surpassed—in many cases I question if they have been equalled in France or any other country. But French actors, I believe, have the same more or less contemptuous feeling about the acting of other nations as they have in regard to the English stage ; they are ridiculously self-conscious in regard to French art, and particularly in regard to the stage. One of the most supremely happy men in this respect is certainly Monsieur Coquelin ; nevertheless I maintain that the English histrionic record is quite equal, in some respects superior, to that of France, one of whose great dramatic authors, by the way, even goes the length of pooh-poohing Shakspere ! The American Donnelly dares to say that Shakspere did not write his plays ; but French jealousy goes a little further ; for Sardou as good as says they were not worth writing. But to get back to what I was saying about remarkable instances of English acting in our own day, let me recall some of them. Take Edward Terry, he used to play ' Bumble ' to my ' Artful Dodger ' in *Oliver Twist*, when I first met him in Belfast ; we all know of his gradual rise since then, and have enjoyed his unique fun and humour on the stage ; I don't remember anything more artistic in its line than his burlesque song in one of the Gaiety pieces about the Bodega ; the tune was an old Welsh air ; his grotesque performance of ' The King of Toledo ' in Byron's burlesque *The Pilgrim of Love*, at the Strand, could not have been surpassed, and as much may be said for many of his other quaint, dry characteristic performances.

" Then there are David James's ' Butterman ' in *Our Boys ;* his ' Boatman ' in *The Guv'nor*—with its catching salutation, ' Your 'and, guv'nor, your 'and ;' Thorne's ' Caleb Deecie,' and later his

'Parson Adams'—true, quaint and natural. What could have been finer in its way, or a more truthful impersonation than Warner's 'Coupeau' in *Drink*; what more terribly realistic than his death-scene?

MR. JOHN CLAYTON IN "ALL FOR HER."

Then poor Clayton's finished and romantic performance in *All for Her;* what a contrast to his acting as the 'Dean' in *Dandy Dick!* I never saw him in *Great Expectations*, but it was in this piece that he made his first marked impression upon critical London. I do not expect to see anything better than his performances in the three plays I have mentioned, all so different, each showing such remarkable versatility.

" Beerbohm Tree is comparatively a new actor; his 'Curate' in *The Private Secretary* and his French conspirator in *Called Back*, great contrasts, were both rare examples of a remarkable talent, and could not, I think, be outmatched. I shall always remember Terriss in the part of the young hero in *Louis the Eleventh* as quite up to the demands of that character, especially for the way in which he wore his armour—no easy thing to do—his brave and gallant bearing, and his great scene with Irving, where he attacks the king in the bedchamber. A breezy actor of sailors and melodramatic heroes demanded by modern Adelphi audiences—not the kind of melodrama we admired twenty years ago, but first-rate no doubt of its class—and I don't know a more free-and-easy dashing hero than Terriss as the virtuous young handsome rescuer of betrayed innocence. Willard now is an actor of another stamp, a young man of experience trained in the last days of provincial stock companies. Could the French stage give us a more perfect bit of work than that of the 'Spider' in *The Silver King*, or a more masterly imper- sonation of its kind than Willard's performance in

Arkwright's Wife? Mr. H. Kemble is another notable comedian and character-actor of a rare humour. He reminds me of Keeley. He had a long turn in the provinces when Willard and Leonard Boyne were serving their apprenticeships, and, as I said before, at the fag-end of the system of stock companies.

" Kemble's impersonation of a gay, impecunious yeomanry officer in Coghlan's *Enemies* was a study that in itself told the whole story of its provincial surroundings ; and in the same play there was a scene between Fernandez and Coghlan that no one who saw it will ever forget for its intense reality. Coghlan's over-trained athlete in *Man and Wife* is becoming a stage memory, even in the actor's lifetime, and before he has ceased to play youthful stage heroes. But talking of theatrical memories, Walter Lacy as ' Don Saluste ' in *Ruy Blas* was a superb performance, sharing all the honours with the hero of the romance, played by Fechter.

" Could anything be more admirable than the ' Carker ' of Fernandez in *Dombey and Son?* And what a reciter he is !—which, by the way, reminds me of the clean-cut, well-finished work of Mrs. Billington, who has so much power and so much tenderness. Giddens has a gift of his own in this way ; his ' American Dutchmen ' are inimitable. One might fill a chapter with examples of the current work of our best actors in merely giving instances of memorable scenes in notable plays. Charles Wyndham's 'Rover' in *Wild*

MR GEORGE HONEY.

Oats is a delightful bit of light comedy, and Germany and Russia have endorsed his 'David Garrick' with Imperial approval. Henry Neville's 'Clancarthy' and his 'Ticket-of-Leave Man' are fine contrasts of study—a clever actor Neville, in

the romantic Don Cæsar de Bazan class of character. Brough in 'Tony Lumpkin' and other
comedy parts is first-rate. I thought Marius's
'Jim the Penman' a remarkable piece of acting,
especially for an artist who is associated more with
burlesque than with serious drama.

"Wilson Barrett¹ in *The Silver King* and *Ben-*

---

¹ Mr. J. S. Wood sends the chronicler the following capital
story, the facts of which have been endorsed in a kindly letter
from Mr. Barrett, and acknowledged with a hearty laugh by
Mr. Toole

"It happened at 'Ye Olde Englishe Fayre,' which I
organized in '81 at the Albert Hall, and I was reminded of
the story only recently by Mr. Wilson Barrett, who, with Mr.
Toole, were the chief actors in this little comedy. W. B. was
to play in *The Clerical Error*, in the West Theatre, and was
dressed before time, and stood by the door on the corridor
floor, which is always very dark. J. L. T. approaches—he
also was to do something—along the bewildering corridor, and
seeing a clerical gentleman standing in the shadow of the
door, asked, ' if that was the best way to the West Theatre,'
when a conversation something like this occurred : 'Theatre,
sir?' says Barrett, recognizing Toole, and disguising his own
voice. 'Yes, sir,' responds Toole. 'I believe there is a
theatre somewhere here, may I venture to inquire the name of
the gentleman whom I am addressing.' 'My name is Toole,'
says the comedian. 'What, Toole the play-actor,' asked
Barrett, with an expression of pained surprise. 'Yes, J. L.
Toole,' is the reply, ' why do you ask ?' 'And you are Toole,
the comedian !' exclaims Barrett, half turning away. 'Is
Toole the comedian such a horrible person ?" responds Toole
warmly. 'He may not be ; but the so-called profession to
which he belongs is a dreadful one.' 'Dreadful !' exclaims

my-Cree stands upon a high platform, and his
'Chatterton' had in it a special tenderness and
charm. Mrs. Bancroft's 'Polly Eccles' and her
scene with Coghlan in the second act of *Sweet-
hearts* would be hard to beat on any stage. Mrs.
John Wood and Arthur Cecil in *The Milliner's
Bill* is a bit of stage fun I have not seen excelled
in Paris or New York. Was anything ever more
droll than Mrs. Wood's 'Pocahontas,' except her
singing of Burnand's droll ditty, ' His Heart was
True to Poll'? Poor George Honey's 'Eccles'
in *Caste*, and his 'Graves' in *Money* were the per-

Toole, 'dreadful, why dreadful?' 'The theatre, sir, is an
immoral thing; it always has been; I fear it always must be ;
oh, my dear friend, be warned in time. Leave it while you
may yet find the better path !' 'Leave it !' exclaims Toole,
' I don't know who you are, but you must allow me to say you
are a very bigoted, not to say impertinent person.' 'Parson,
sir !' exclaimed Barrett, 'that is the character I am assuming at the moment.' 'Then you are assuming it in a very
offensive manner, sir, and I am sorry to seem rude in making
that remark; I have known and do know many of your cloth,
and have invariably found them men of charity and benevolence, and—' 'That will do Johnny, old friend,' says Barrett,
in his own voice; 'I have made a clerical error, evidently;
you had better get on ; you'll miss your cue ; they have called
you, I believe, ever so long since.' 'Oh, you vagabond !'
exclaims Toole, as he shakes his fellow-actor's hand and
hurries in the direction pointed out to him—not to perdition
but to act for a charity, an occupation which many artists find
congenial and with the result of advancing the interests of
many a good cause."

fection of stage art. Edouin's acting in *Turned Up* is a very funny and interesting bit of low comedy. Mrs. Kendal has no rival in domestic comedy. In her own line she is as supreme as

MISS KATE PHILLIPS.

Miss Terry is in hers, and both are artists worthy of any period and any country. Mrs. Kendal's ' Pauline,' and ' Miss Hardcastle,' and her ' Dora ' in *Diplomacy* are superb impersonations ; while upon the still higher platform of Shaksperian art, Miss Terry's ' Desdemona,' ' Ophelia,' and ' Beatrice ' cannot be surpassed, and I doubt if they have ever been equalled. Bancroft in *Caste* was a very distinguished figure, and his performance of ' Tom Stylus ' in *Society* is fine comedy acting. I need only mention Irving's ' Louis XI.,' ' Charles I.,' ' Shylock,' ' Mathias,' ' Hamlet.'

" When one recalls these actors and scenes, not alone from the past, but chiefly in the present, one is inclined to smile at the notion that we are short of actors, that we are eclipsed by the French stage. And yet I have not mentioned Penley, ~~Arthur Roberts,~~ Blakely, Alexander, Arthur Williams, Brookfield, Alfred Bishop, Miss Emery, the two Miss Rorkes, Harry Nicholls, Miss Fanny Brough, Mr. Yorke Stephens, and others ; and I suppose I am not entitled to count in Mary Anderson, who belongs to America, and yet she seems more and more to belong to us. Nor ought I, perhaps, to mention my own company, but Shelton, as the old lord in *The Butler ;* Ward as the hermit in *Paw Claudian ;* Miss Thorne, as the buxom ' Lady Bootleton ;' Miss Johnstone as ' Tilly Slowboy ;' Miss Lyndon, in *Stage Dora ;* Miss Phillips, in *The Don ;* and Billington, in *Dot*, are quite worthy of the best traditions of the stage. The French companies we have seen of late in London can certainly teach us nothing ; while, I maintain, that we could teach them many things, not only in regard to the exhibition of the variety of the human passions, but in regard to the production of plays.   The best of these miscellaneous companies have the same set of actions as if they had all learnt deportment, fencing, and the rest from the same master.   Sarah Bernhardt is the only French player I have ever seen who did not literally come down to the footlights and talk to the audience.   Even Monsieur Coquelin has this bad habit, and his expressed views of the ' Burgomaster ' in *The Bells* show in him a wonderful lack of that imagination which is considered necessary for the interpretation of characters under the influence of either intense feeling or morbid fancy.   But I am, I fear, entering upon the office of the critic ; and, after all, the French way may be the best for the French audiences—they are different from us, have different views of life, look at the stage from a different standpoint, and may be all right in their way : but if I concede this to them I want the same consideration for us, if not only from themselves, at least from English play-goers and critics.   Monsieur Sardou says *Hamlet* is rubbish, a poor play and badly constructed, and that Shakspere is not a good dramatist.   Monsieur Coquelin maintains that the fear-haunted ' Mathias ' —who under the influence of the mountebank offering to unmask his secret thoughts, he being a murderer, goes home, makes provision against his possible death, and dies of fright of the mesmerist —does not require to be played except as a common ignorant person, and that it is not necessary to suggest anything weird and strange to the audience in the sound of bells by which he is haunted. It seems to me that, in this view of the story of *The Bells*, M. Coquelin is just as wrong as M. Sardou is about *Hamlet* and Shakspere. So far as Sardou is concerned, and in saying this I have only admiration for his great powers as a dramatist, he is as silly and inconsequential about Shakspere as a certain lecturer was in his reply to a juvenile member of his audience as related by Edmund Yates. "Many years ago, one hot summer evening," says my old friend, "I turned into the pit of the Strand Theatre, where were exhibiting a party of Bosjesmen, stunted savages from Africa. I paid sixpence for admission, the price being a shilling to the boxes, and threepence to the gallery. The wretched little beings had gone through a portion of their performance, war-dances, imitation of deer-tracking and shooting, &c., when their showman, a tall, swaggering person in evening dress, with his hair elaborately parted down the middle, advanced to the footlights to give us some particulars about them. 'The little man,' he announced in very mellifluous tones, 'the little man is forty-two years old!' He paused an instant, and a boy in the threepenny gallery called out shrilly, ' And 'ow old are *you?*' There was a laugh, and the showman was disconcerted for a moment. Then, laying his hand on his shirt-front, and breathing hard, he looked up at his little querist and said with much dignity, ' Old enough, sir, to tell you that you are—no gentleman!' "

VI.

" APROPOS of French acting and actors," continued Toole, when he had done chuckling over the Bosjesmen's entertainment, "one might mention, as a pleasant incident, Irving's supper to Madame Sarah Bernhardt, and also the fact that the leading French critics have acknowledged the high excellence of his art. Many of Irving's entertainments in the Beefsteak Club Room are historical, and you have, no doubt, made a note of some of them. None was, however, I think more interesting than the supper he gave to Madame Sarah Bernhardt, on her leaving London for some wonderful tour in Mexico or Africa, or somewhere at the other ends of the earth. It was a distinguished little company, you remember,

of ladies and gentlemen, and the divine Sarah
came direct from the stage of Her Majesty's
after a very arduous performance. What I am
more particularly thinking about was the incident
of Irving describing to us Clint's picture of the
great Kean scene in *A New Way to Pay Old
Debts*—you drew my attention to the singular
likeness there was in the upper part of the heads
of Kean, Irving, and Bernhardt. Irving acting
as showman to Ellen Terry and Sarah Bernhardt, before the picture of Edmund Kean
as 'Sir Giles Overreach,' would make a fine
historical picture. What a graceful little speech
Irving made, in proposing Sarah Bernhardt's
health!"

"And what a happy speech you made," I
replied, "in giving the toast of 'our leading
English actress, Ellen Terry,' whose 'Margaret,'
'Ophelia,' and 'Olivia,' you mentioned as being
'poetic as they are womanly!' It was indeed an
interesting occasion."

"And what a prince Irving is in making these
occasions! I am very glad to hear that he had
an exceptional experience on a recent visit to
Paris. Some of the leading men of the theatres
received him most kindly, and also with distinction. This is as it should be. Our French friends
honour their calling when they honour Irving,

and a little reciprocity in the way of professional courtesy is delightful!

"I have several times played with Irving for benefits, once or twice at his own theatre. Once we did *Robert Macaire*. We rollicked through

MR. TOOLE AS "JACQUE STROP."

it. It was as much fun to us as I hope it was to the audience. I was 'Jacques Strop.' Well, you know what a couple of exaggerated impecunious ruffians we looked. I could not help thinking how incongruous a certain conversation which we had would have seemed to an outsider. It was a question of making up the amount of the sum for the fund of which we were playing to a thousand pounds. It was at the close of the piece—a hurried little chat. 'About a hundred and fifty pounds short of a thousand,' said Robert Macaire, 'I think we ought to make it up a thousand.' 'By all means,' said Jacques Strop, who had only a minute or two before sneaked off in custody. 'I'll give so much,' said Robert. 'And I'll give so much, too,' I said ; and then it seemed as if we were practising a duet which Grossmith wrote for me, 'I was a sailor as a boy ; and I was a sailor too !' I couldn't help roaring with laughter as the notion struck me. 'What is it ?' said Robert Macaire, this time very much like Irving. 'Nothing, it's all right,' I said. And we made it a thousand pounds, we two ragamuffins, and it was delightful to hear the round upon round of applause when the sum to be handed over to the fund in question was mentioned to the house."

VIII.

"THE BEST OF FRIENDS MUST PART."

Management—The Folly—New plays—Toole's Theatre—
    Between then and now—Dramatic authors and their
    methods—Byron, Burnand, Pinero, Merivale—Taverns
    and clubs—The Garrick and the Green-room—The Prince
    of Wales and how he kept a secret—Reminiscences of
    Sandringham—Meeting the Queen at Invercauld—The
    late Prince Imperial—Some anecdotes of Byron—
    Parting words.

I.

"WE have been chatting for the past two hours about everything and everybody," I said, "and we have not yet picked up the thread of our story from the point of your return from America."

"Then let us return, as you novelists say, to the period where we left our hero, on his triumphant home-coming from the vast continent of America, eh?"

With the aid of memoranda of my own, including a date or two, and one of Mr. Lowne's scrap-books, my host gave me the following particulars of his work, bringing our joint labours down to the present time :—

"On my return from America I went on tour in the provinces before I came back to town. But you must let me digress a moment. The notes you have given me suggest points I must not forget.

"Every foot of ground in London, more particularly about Charing Cross, may be called both sacred and historic. But we will not go back to that, eh? It might be thought too learned for a comedian to rake up the history of Charing Cross.

"I found myself wandering into a very distant time the other night, when I was thinking about the questions you asked me concerning the Folly Theatre. I had visions of the Cross of Charing, and all the gay and warlike doings that belong to its early history. Our friend Irving could put those wonderful scenes upon his stage, and he has plenty of warrant in Shakspere; but we must be content with more modern work. What made me begin to think of historic and sacred ground was the fact that only comparatively a few years ago the site of this theatre was occupied by a Roman Catholic oratory, where two popular fathers attracted goodly audiences—I mean congregations. I do not know why they disappeared or how, but upon the foundations of the oratory arose the Polygraphic Hall, which afterwards became known as the Charing Cross Theatre, at which Woodin gave his various performances. Some alterations and improvements were afterwards made, and it became the Folly Theatre, which eventually came into my hands.

"Some people were inclined to christen it 'Toole's Folly.' They thought a popular actor who could always get a good starring engagement, with or without his own company, was not quite wise in entering upon management on his own account. But I felt the time had come when I ought to have a house of my own; and it was not, after all, a very daring stroke of ambition to take the Folly Theatre. So when I returned from America, after making a short but very successful provincial tour, I settled down at the Folly a full-blown London manager. I had the little theatre re-decorated, made the most of its resources, and opened very prosperously with Byron's capital farcical comedy, *A Fool and His Money*, followed by *Ici on Parle Français*.

"This was in 1879. I had originally produced, as previously mentioned, *A Fool and His Money*, at the Globe Theatre, nearly two years previously. The revival went admirably, and in the livery of 'Chawles," responding to very loud applause and calls for a speech, I thanked my very genial audience, told them I was not in a position to make an eloquent speech, that I had been too busy to think one out, but ventured to say there was no knowing what might occur in the course of the season. At the same time I promised them a new comedy by Mr. Byron, whose name was received with a genuine burst of hearty applause. After I had said these few words there was a call for Byron, who came forward and received quite an ovation. So you see my managerial reign began pleasantly, and I do not think it has ever justified the cynical suggestion that the Charing Cross venture might be called 'Toole's Folly.' The Press was exceedingly kind : my welcome home from America was as hearty in the newspapers as it was in the theatre.

" During an illness that followed, and a sad domestic affliction, Byron came to my assistance with a revival of *Not Such a Fool as He Looks ; or, Sir Simon Simple*, playing the leading part himself, and having excellent support from my company, Mr. Westland taking my part of 'Spriggins' in the after-piece.

" *Married in Haste* and *Cyril's Success* were also revived ; and I returned in the first week of February, played *Paul Pry*, *Domestic Economy*, and *A Fool and His Money*, and on the last night in March, 1880, produced *The Upper Crust*, by Byron, with

Billington as 'Lord Hesketh,' Mr. E. W. Garden as 'Sir Robert Boobleton, Bart.,' Mr. E. D. Ward as 'Walter Wrentmore,' Mr. T. Sidney as 'Tibworth,' Miss Lilian Cavallier as 'Norah Doublechick,' Miss Rowland Phillips as 'Kate Vennemore,' Miss Emily Thorn as 'Lady Boobleton,' and myself as 'Mr. Barnaby Doublechick,' proprietor of Doublechick's Diaphanous Soap. I do not think Byron was ever happier in his dialogue, which was both sparkling and humorous, while his sketches of 'Doublechick' and 'Boobleton' were quite in his most humorous vein. The comedy was a great success: it had a long run.

"In the summer season we added to the programme a pretty little comedy by Mr. A. W. Pinero, called *Hester's Mystery*. This was one of the first pieces from Mr. Pinero's delightful pen. The first thing, I believe, he ever did was *The Money-spinner*, produced in the country, and purchased there by Mr. Kendal. Pinero, who was a member of the Lyceum company, was introduced to me as a dramatist by Irving.

"In the autumn of that year I gave a few matinées, reviving *Dot*, and introducing later Mr. Byron's *The Light Fantastic*, which went so well that I transferred it to the evening bill. I played a dancing-master, called 'Professor

Slithery.'   The piece was very farcical, and went with roars of laughter.

" *The Upper Crust* went merrily along into the next year, when I changed the after-piece from *The Light Fantastic* to Robert Reece's *Wizard of the Wilderness*, originally played at the Gaiety in March, 1873.   I was ' Didymus Dexter,' a conjuring chemist, and introduced some sleight-of-hand tricks, for which purpose I took lessons of a professional magician, who was very much bothered now and then, when sitting in front, at my occasional forgetfulness or inefficiency, more particularly that when I spoiled a trick I ' guyed ' it and made fun of it.

" In June, 1881, when *The Upper Crust* had run over four hundred nights, I produced Mr. Burnand's *Artful Cards*, which had been very successful during my Gaiety engagement, and I ran it during alternate nights with *The Upper Crust*, following it by a comedy by Mrs. Fairbairn, called *Waiting Consent*, in which Mr. Elmore, Mr. Ward, Mr. Shelton, and Miss Rowland Phillips appeared.

" In the middle of July I gave two farewell performances prior to closing my initial season of management, taking a rest, and arranging for my provincial tour.   On Friday evening, July 22nd, 1881, the programme opened with *Hester's*

Mystery, followed by *The Pretty Horsebreaker*, a scene from *The Wife*, the sketch of *Trying a Magistrate*, a new farce by Sydney Grundy, called *Over the Garden Wall*, the whole concluding with the so-called diverting absurdity, entitled *Welsh Rabbits*. Miss Fanny Josephs and Mr. Billington appeared with me in *The Pretty Horsebreaker*, and Mr. John McCulloch, the well-known American tragedian, and Mr. James Fernandez appeared in *The Wife*.

"Called upon for a few words, I mentioned that the season had lasted twenty-one months, and had been so very successful that I had been induced to take the Folly on a long lease, and intended to make the house very comfortable for my reappearance in December. I thanked my fellow-artists who had assisted me ; and, *à propos* of the assistance of Mr. Irving and Miss Terry for the following morning, I expressed a hope that I should return the compliment to the Lyceum Manager by playing for his benefit the next evening in the farce called *The Birthplace of Podgers*, which was first represented at the Lyceum twenty-three years previously, when that house was managed by the late Mr. Charles Dillon. I mentioned the story we have told in a previous chapter, that *The Birthplace of Podgers* was introduced to me by Mr. Edmund Yates, with the declaration that the author, Mr. John Hollingshead, would never leave me until the farce was produced. That author never did leave me, as you know, until that event occurred ; and I was then residing, as I told the audience, in a house which was afterwards pulled

MR. TOOLE AS "TOM CRANKEY" IN "THE BIRTHPLACE OF PODGERS."

down to make way for the Strand Music Hall, subsequently converted into the Gaiety Theatre under the auspices of Mr. Hollingshead, who had followed me up with such good and friendly results. 'Friend John' little thought, as a hard-working journalist in those days, that he would come to be manager and chief proprietor of a popular theatre built on the site of the room where we discussed *The Birthplace of Podgers.*

" On the next evening my farewell programme included *The Hunchback*, with Ellen Terry as ' Helen,' and Henry Irving as ' Modus.' Mr. Arthur Sketchley gave his *Experiences of Mrs. Brown at the Play;* we also did *Domestic Economy;* and Mr. Grundy's little farce of *Over the Garden Wall* went with roars of laughter.   In that I was ' Mr. Folgate,' my mind and peace disturbed by the cat of my next-door neighbour, ' Mr. Bartholomew Close.'   I determined to take the life of my feline foe, but, instead of shooting the cat, knocked over the gardener, out of which a good many ridiculous complications arose."

II.

" I RETURNED to Charing Cross in December, the alterations in the theatre occupying more time than I had anticipated, and costing me, one way and another, upwards of ten thousand pounds.   I decided to call the house ' Toole's Theatre,' and re-opened it under that title on the 16th February, 1882.   The house was much enlarged, very prettily decorated, boasted a handsome saloon, staircase, and *foyer*, a fine hall, and was altogether, as it is to-day, a very charming, pretty little house. The newspaper descriptions of the artistic character of its decorations were elaborate, and, to me, most interesting. I confess I was a little surprised to find that my decorations were Raphaelesque, that my new ceiling was in the Rénaissance style, my saloon Pompeian ; but altogether I was very delighted with everything and everybody about the place, and shall not in a hurry forget the hearty reception which a crowded audience gave me on my return in February, 1882.

" I opened the new house, 'Toole's,' with *Paul Pry* and *Domestic Economy*, and on the fall of the curtain, being called upon for a speech, I made one, and am enabled to give it to you, if not quite verbatim, quite near enough. The newspapers, in reporting speeches, know how to separate the wheat from the chaff, and this is one of the few examples of their skill in this respect that I have by me :—

" 'It was expected,' he said, ' that he should have a " few words " with the audience ; but that had a very alarming sound, as though he and they were going to quarrel, a thing which they had never done, and which he hoped they never would do. (Cheers and laughter.) He was much obliged to them for coming to visit him in his new home, and he was glad to see them all looking so well.

(Laughter.)   He protested that he thought they looked better than they would at any other theatre —(laughter)—and the oftener they came there the better they would continue to look. (Laughter.) It was to be hoped that they would appreciate the disinterested spirit in which he made these remarks. (Laughter.)   His time had been so fully occupied that he had not had leisure to prepare a speech, but he trusted they would give him credit for all the pretty things he ought to say, Above all, he hoped that they liked the theatre. (Cheers.) If anybody had any complaint—he did not mean indisposition—he requested that a line might be dropped to him, and the grievance should be rectified. (Cheers.) The theatre had its 'exits and its entrances,' as Shakespeare would say, and many of them ; and not only had ample provision been made against fire, but a verandah had been erected in front to protect them from water as well. (Laughter.)   In the course of the evening he had received many telegrams from friends— Mr. Irving, Mr. Byron, and Mr. Sims Reeves in the number—wishing him success, and he was gratefully sensible of the kindness he had experienced from all quarters. In conclusion, he again thanked the audience for their hearty reception, and expressed a hope that the friendly relations which had always existed between him and the public would remain unclouded to the last.' "

III.

" I would like to mention my indebtedness to my friend Mr. J. C. Parkinson for his practical and sympathetic advice in connection with the lesseeship, re-construction, and re-naming of the Folly Theatre, to me a very important enterprise. It is a great privilege, in one's serious undertakings, to have the clear-headed and disinterested counsel of such a friend as Parkinson.

" The Folly was a poor little house, but it had possibilities, and to-day it is one of the prettiest theatres, and " (with a laugh) " one of the plea-santest theatres I have ever played in. How one gets to like what belongs to oneself! I kept to-gether my stock company, which is one of the few stock companies now existing ; I mean by that, the members of it are not merely engaged for the run of a piece, but are with me all the year round. I have to make occasional changes, of course; but Billington, Miss Lyndon, Miss Johnstone, Mr. Shelton, Mr. Gardner, Mr. Westland, Mr. Ward, Miss Thorne, and Mr. Lowne have been my companions, some of them for many years ; Ward has left me for

America, Gardner has gone to the Adelphi. Mr. Cortly, and Miss Phillips are new comers; but what I wanted to point out is that my com-

MR. JOHN BILLINGTON.

pany is formed and maintained on the old stock principle, and they have had parts written for them by Byron, Burnand, Merivale, Pinero, and other authors, in several of my best original comedies.

"I find it pleasant to see the same faces year after year, and most valuable to be working with the same artists. There can hardly be a happier family than we are, myself and company, always on excellent terms on and off the stage, in business ever anxious to do our best with any piece in which we are engaged. The principal works I had played up to this time were written by Byron. Poor fellow, he had most endearing qualities, and a wonderful fund of humour; his fun was always genial, never coarse, never cruel, he was more than a wit, he was a true humorist; and this can also be said of Burnand, and what a delightful thing is humour without a sting; wit rarely, I think, is without it, I mean wit by itself. There is point enough in the humour of Burnand and Byron, and both men have their sparkle and their pungency, a trifle of bitter, and as Spriggins would say, a *soupçon* of acid; but neither their wit nor their humour ever leaves a wound behind, while their laughter is hearty and thoroughly honest."

IV.

"THE most notable event of this first season of the newly-named house in King William Street was the production of a three-act play by Byron, entitled *Auntie*. It began with rather a bad omen : a portion of the scenery took fire in the first act. There was a little scare for a few minutes, but Ward, Billington, and myself reassured the audience : a fireman opened the extra door in the pit, and while the stage carpenters were putting out the little conflagration, which was seen at once to be only a small affair, I walked down to the footlights and assured the house that there were eight or nine fire-engines and eighty or ninety firemen in constant readiness for incidents of this kind, and begged they would not be alarmed, but wait and enjoy Mr. Byron's play, into which it had not been intended to introduce anything alarming. *Auntie* was not one of Byron's most successful efforts, but it had a prosperous little run.

" At the close of the season I made another provincial tour, letting the theatre for the summer and early autumn season to Miss Fanny Davenport ; and, returning from the provinces in October, re-opened with *The Upper Crust*, and *Guffin's Elopement*, by Mr. Arthur Law and Mr. George Grossmith, sang ' The Speaker's Eye,' and produced Pinero's *Girls and Boys*, a clever English comedy, full of original thoughts and suggestions, about which great interest was felt, more particularly as it followed *The Squire*, at the St. James's, which had caused considerable controversy. *Girls and Boys* was either too clever or not clever enough, but it did not succeed in

MR. TOOLE IN "STAGE DORA."

pleasing the public, and in the spring I revived *Uncle Dick's Darling*, with Billington as ' Chevenix ' and Miss Florence West as ' Mary Belton,' in which this young lady made a promising first appearance on the regular stage.

"I followed *Uncle Dick* with *Artful Cards*, and on the 27th May produced Burnand's admirable burlesque of *Fedora*, in which Miss Marie Linden quite took the town in her successful imitation of Sarah Bernhardt. Oddly enough she had not seen the great French actress, but had studied her through the performance of Mrs. Bernard Beere, making-up, however, from photographs of the original French heroine. The burlesque hit the public at once, and was pronounced by the critics to be one of the cleverest and most mirthful of Burnand's many lively productions.

"This year I let the theatre during my provincial tours to Mr. T. W. Robertson, who produced with good success a round of the Robertsonian comedies.

"Early in 1884, Mr. Burnand followed up his success with *Fedora* by a genial travesty of Mr. Wilson Barrett's very successful production of *Claudian*. The piece was called *Paw Clawdian*, Miss Marie Linden being as successful in her imitation of Miss Eastlake as she had been previously in regard to Sarah Bernhardt, Mr. E. D. Ward making a hit as a burlesque Wilson Barrett in the part of the Hermit.

"We are now getting too near the present time, which is making its own history in the very presence of the reader, to go into minute details about one's other work. Between the production of *Paw Clawdian* and to-day I have gone on the same round of new productions, provincial tours, and attacks of the gout, the latter introducing me

MR. TOOLE AS "THE BUTLER."

to Aix, and giving me evidence of much kindly feeling on the part of the public, and touching proofs of many old and true friendships. The leading incidents of ' Toole's ' in these days are the production of *Going It*, by the veteran playwright,

Mr. Madison Morton ; a burlesque of the Lyceum *Faust*, by Burnand ; *The Butler*, by Mr. and Mrs. Herman Merivale ; and *The Don*, by the same authors. These two plays have taken a foremost place among my most successful pieces, and *The Don* has had an exceptional recognition in the two great University cities.[1] When I went to play the piece at Oxford a little party of real Dons invited me to luncheon, and I need not tell you how

[1] " Mr. Toole has reason to be proud of himself as the Dean of Chapels in *The Don*. The two University towns and cities have endorsed the verdict of London. They may be said to have conferred honorary degrees on *The Don*. Cambridge having received the comedy with unanimous favour ; at Oxford, on Thursday, the new theatre was crowded with a fashionable audience. Many heads of colleges, professors, undergraduates, pretty women, and well-known citizens were present ; and every point that more especially illustrated college life, or made honest fun of it during Commemoration time, met with ripples of laughter, which occasionally broke out into rounds of applause. It says much for the broad liberality of modern Oxford when the players are so well received, and that even the classic gown and almost sacred cap may be used without giving offence, the comedy being wholesome, and of good, honest humour. There are still managers and playwrights who think the public like what they call ' a little spice ' in stage merriment ; but the best plays and the most popular are those to which Paterfamilias can take his family, and *The Don* is one of those honest, genial pieces. Mr. Toole throughout his career has never given his audiences the smallest cause of offence in regard to what he has put upon the stage, or how he has put it on, and one cannot but rejoice at his continued success."— *Sunday Times*, June 10th, 1888.

complimentary they were to me and to the profession to which I belong, for you were present, and I am sure the reader will believe me when I say that in all the flattering recognition I have received from distinguished men and famous audiences I feel grateful, not simply for myself alone, but for the profession at large, a profession of which I feel very proud, and a profession which, rightly understood, is one of great public usefulness, not only as a matter of entertainment, but as a factor in the public work of national education."

V.

"COMING back for a moment to authors, I recall with much delight remembrances of the pleasant intercourse I have had with many of them, more especially with those who have written for me. Poor Byron! the day he was buried I played 'Chawles' at the Crystal Palace; I could not help it, one is obliged to keep one's engagements; but I felt very sad. It seemed to me once or twice as if I could hear the funeral service while I was speaking the dear fellow's merry lines. Byron wrote for me *The Upper Crust, A Fool and His Money, Auntie, The Light Fantastic, Uncle Dick's Darling*, and *Tottles*. Burnand has fitted me, as they call it, with *Paw Claudian*,

Stage Dora, and *Artful Cards*, and I think the two first mentioned are among the cleverest of his many humorous burlesques.

"While Byron and Burnand had many points in common, and are more or less akin in their work, their stage management was very opposite. Byron used to take things very easy ; would make a suggestion, or drop a hint, and then disappear, glide away, so to speak.   On the other hand, Burnand will work up his scenes at rehearsal in the most wonderful way ; follow up an idea, or jump at a new suggestion, and stick to it persistently until he has developed it into the shape it has taken in his mind.   Pinero is very patient and careful in the stage-managing of his plays ; his *Girls and Boys* seemed to me to be an admirable play ; but it did not run for some reason or other.   It was capitally staged by Pinero, whose *Hester's Mystery* is one of my best little stock pieces ; although one of the first things he ever wrote, it showed his delicate and artistic method, and I think the public is fortunate in having such a writer among its servants.   In these days, when there is supposed to be a prurient tendency in public taste, which, however, I am inclined to deny, it is very satisfactory to be able to point to the successes of Burnand and Byron in the realm of comedy and burlesque, and of Pinero and Merivale as play-wrights who have contributed to the stage farcical comedy, as well as comedy and drama of the highest class.

" I have not for many years played any character that has given me more personal pleasure as an actor than *The Don*.   In *The Butler* and *The Don* I have had valuable assistance from one of the newest members of my company, Miss Phillips.   In regard to the method of dramatists, it is worth mentioning, perhaps, that Byron rarely had to cut his manuscript; he worked it into the right proportions as to length before the theatre ever saw it; but Merivale is very fertile as an author. He elaborates immensely.   In one of his pieces there always seems to me at the outset to be enough matter for two.   It was a great surprise to me to discover that a dramatist of so poetic a turn of mind as Merivale should have in him so much real fun as is shown in both *The Butler* and *The Don*."

VI.

" WHEN we were talking of actors and acting just now, I meant to say something about clubs; it is quite *à propos*."

"I am all attention," I said.

"The young actor of the present day," continued Toole, "has many pleasant social advantages not to be had in my early days. I count most prominently among these the modern club. I don't of course mean the Garrick, because it is not only necessary that a man should belong to the profession to be an acceptable member of the Garrick, but he must have made his mark, not only before the public, but among his professional friends. The Garrick, therefore, gives an actor a sort of endorsement of character and ability, a kind of diploma, as it were. But there are on the way up to the Garrick various minor clubs, where men can meet each other in a pleasant way, not only for social purposes, but to talk and chat and exchange notes and opinions about their art. In my early days the tavern was almost the only place where actors could meet, and there they were not always able to select their company. In these days there are many artistic clubs where actors meet authors, journalists, artists, and others who are in sympathy with the stage, many of them, as dramatic authors, connected with it; and this kind of meeting has, I venture to think, a far more elevating effect upon the status and ambition of the actor than the old tavern days when I was a boy. The Green-room, I suppose, is more particularly the actor's club to-day. There are, of

course, the Savage, the Arundel, the Whitefriars,
and other clubs where actors are welcome, and in
connection with which one has pleasant memories,
but the Green-room seems to me to be particularly an actors' club, and it is very pleasant, after
a night's work, to meet the men of one's own
craft over a glass of wine or a hand at whist. The
Garrick entered upon quite a new phase of social
life a few years ago, when we arranged the Saturday night suppers to which members can invite
their friends, members and guests supping together in common. We hear a great deal about
the brilliant days of the Garrick, the rare smoking-
room chat when Jerrold, Thackeray, and others
were members ; but I don't think they could have
had much pleasanter times than we have at the
Garrick now. They certainly had not the number of guests and members sitting down together
that we have on Saturday nights. One may not,
I conclude, describe any of these club gatherings ;
but some of them will make history. I don't
know whether there are diarists among us who
make notes of Garrick evenings for future reminiscences ; but I shouldn't wonder that a hundred
years hence, if we could revisit the glimpses of
the moon, some of us will be much more celebrated in biographies, reminiscences, diaries, and
in other historical works, than we are now."

"You said the other day that I ought to say something about the Prince of Wales. I wish we might both think it in good taste to say all I feel about him, not only as a prince, not only as the heir to the throne, but as a man and a patron of art. No prince has ever shown so much delicate, manly, kindly consideration for the members of my profession, and, from all I hear in the country and in town, he is just as popular with the other professions. In the country it is delightful to hear men who hunt and shoot, and carry on the sporting traditions of England, talk of the Prince, not only as a host, but as a guest; not only as a shot, but as a fearless rider across country. Of course, it would not become me to say more than this. One cannot praise a prince—one leaves mere courtiers to do that—but if I am taken to the Tower and beheaded for undue familiarity, I cannot help saying that I think him, apart from his Royal status, a really excellent gentleman, a pleasant companion, and a most delightful host. He has a keen sense of fun. When first he asked me to go down to Sandringham and act, he wanted to make the occasion a surprise for the Princess and his friends. Loveday had to go down and make certain preliminary arrangements. The Prince explained that he wished him to keep his business at Sandringham a close secret, 'and,' his Royal Highness added, 'to enable you to do so I shall introduce you as the Spanish Ambas-

THE PRINCE AND THE "SPANISH AMBASSADOR."

sador!' 'Oh, but I cannot speak Spanish, sir!' said Loveday. 'Nor can they,' said the Prince, laughing; 'so your disguise will be perfect.'

"We played in a fit-up in the Bowling Alley, the programme being *Our Clerks, The Steeple-chase,* and *Ici on parle Français.* At the close of the performance we supped together in the dining-hall, and after supper our Royal host and his brothers, Prince Leopold and the Duke of Connaught, joined us, with several of the Prince's guests.   The Prince proposed my health in a very genial and kindly speech, and we spent a most agreeable time.

"I have played with my company three times at Sandringham.   On the second occasion the stage was erected in the ball-room, a lovely apartment ; we had a proper proscenium, and everything in order.   The occasion was the twenty-first birthday of Prince Victor.   We played *Paul Pry*, *Guffin's Elopement*, and I sang 'The Speaker's Eye.'   The Royal and distinguished audience numbered from three to four hundred, and I never played before a more enthusiastic house.   They took every point, and both laughed and applauded heartily.   There is an idea, I fancy, among some people, that it is not etiquette to enjoy yourself too much in the presence of Royalty.   I can only say that it is not my experience ; I never heard heartier laughter than at Sandringham, nor, under its influence, I think, ever played with greater enjoyment ; and I believe every member of my company felt the same.   On our third visit to Sandringham we played *Going It* and *The Birthplace of Podgers*.

" I think I may say, without being impertinent, that there is something very winning in the Prince's manners, and he is very considerate and happy in his courtesies. Her Royal Highness the Princess of Wales is as unaffected as she is gracious, and altogether I should think the Sandringham household is a model of domestic peace and happiness. It is the type of the best English life, and the host and hostess seem to be inspired in all they do by the best English traditions."

VIII.

" I AM reminded, while speaking of the Prince, of an incident of my being somewhat nervous in the presence of Royalty in Scotland. Colonel Farquharson had often invited me to visit him at Invercauld, a lovely place a little beyond Balmoral. I had much wished to do so, but for a long time no opportunity offered. At last I was playing at Aberdeen, when what is called ' a preaching night ' intervened, and gave me a night off. I telegraphed Colonel Farquharson to this effect, and said I had a couple of friends with me : they were Lowne and my manager, Loveday. He replied, ' Bring them, and come to Invercauld ; shall be delighted to receive you.'

" We travelled to Ballater by rail, and from

thence we drove to Invercauld. We had just passed Abergeldie, the Prince's place, when, in a very narrow road, we met Her Majesty walking with one or two of her sons, and attended by several gillies. The Queen had to stop for us to go by. We uncovered and paid all due respect and reverence to Her Majesty, who smiled, bowed, and we went on our way.

"At Invercauld, after luncheon, we went out on ponies, attended by gillies. We had not gone very far when one of the party said, 'Here's Her Majesty coming!' and, sure enough, the Queen came along. This time she was driving. It was now our turn to stand aside while the Queen passed us, and the gillies gracefully reined up their steeds. I am not much of a horseman; I tried, however, to imitate one to the best of my ability; thought of Mazeppa and other performers of my youth, and felt a little uncertain as to my powers of reining in a Scotch pony. However, I did my best; as also did Lowne and Loveday. The Queen smiled, and I am sure she must have thought we were three awful guys.

"We were invited to chase the wild deer, but ventured to decline this mark of hospitality, although I brought home with me several fine examples of big game, one of which, of course, you've noticed in the hall, and there is another at the theatre.   Unsophisticated guests of mine are sometimes induced to believe that they are reminiscences of my sporting proclivities; but some people never seem quite to understand when you are joking and when you are not.   It was no joke reining up that spirited pony at Invercauld in the presence of Royalty, I can tell you."

IX.

" I RECALL an interesting little party given by Mr. Gilbert Farquhar, at the office of Bell's Telephone, in Cannon Street, in March, 1878.   That was the first great public test, if you remember, of the telephone in this country.   The wire was laid to Windsor, and the Queen graciously condescended to preside over these first popular manifestations. The party at our end of the telephone, in Cannon Street, included the late Prince Imperial, who came up from Chislehurst for the occasion; the Duchess of Westminster and daughter ; the Countess De la Warr, the Marchesa Sauturée, Mrs. Langtry, Mrs. Cornwallis West, Lord Dorchester, Lady D. Neville, Lord De Clifford, Mr. Hamilton Aide, and Miss Kate Field—who, by the way, was personally interested in the business features of Bell's Telephone.   She sang a ballad for the Royal ear, and I was induced to speak a little French from a certain popular comedy of mine.

" The Prince Imperial, a very charming and interesting young fellow, came to the Gaiety a few nights afterwards to see me in *Ici on parle Français*, and was brought round to my room, where we had a pleasant chat. He said he had come to take a lesson in French, and was very genial and unaffected."

X.

' DURING his illness poor Byron was staying at Hastings, having a quiet, lazy, reflective time. I used to send him curious parcels of things. I happened to be in Nottingham Market-Place, and bought him all kinds of samples of everything out of the market, making up a miscellaneous hamper. I knew that it would amuse him to unpack them. The incongruity of the contents would tickle his fancy, and I always put in a few trifles that might be useful to the landlady. Every little cheap thing in the market I think I purchased one day. I had a charming letter from him, describing the unpacking of the hamper, his own amusement, and the delight of the landlady, to whose *cuisine* I at least added variety.

"In this letter he spoke of his languor and lassitude, his desire for quiet, and of the narrow escape he had had of a visit from a sort of physical thunderbolt. He was sitting at the window, looking through the venetian blinds, when he saw C—— enter the gate in front, just in time to say he was not at home; otherwise the next moment there would have been, as he said, a sort of Punch-and-Judy-man business — a thundering knock at the door, a rush and tramp, a tramp and rush, upstairs into his room, a tremendous, vigorous shake of the hand, and a loud, cheery, noisy voice shouting, 'Rooty-too! Here we are! How are you, my boy! Glad to find you: only just heard you were in Hastings,' &c.

" He said he had been reading the local newspaper, and was very much amused with the criticism of the theatre, in which the writer said Miss Sarah Thorne's *Wages of Sin* was a little too heavy for Hastings.

" Poor Byron! most of his good things have been printed; but you were speaking of the spontaneity of his wit and the geniality of his humour. I don't remember any new illustration of this, except a very small one; but it is very characteristic of our dear old friend. It was the very week before he died. I was sitting by his bed, when Mrs. Byron said, ' So-and-So has called for a character.' The So-and-So was a man-servant, who had lived with him some years. Byron was talking business with me, and was a trifle impatient. 'I did not want to be disturbed just now,' he said; 'I am willing to give him a character, of course, but what sort of a character does he want, a bad one or a good one?' He turned to me and smiled as he asked this question, and as he did when answering an application from his groom, who reported that one of his horses was ill—should he give it a ball—he wrote, 'Yes, give it a ball, but don't ask too many.'

"I remember once calling for Byron at the Criterion Theatre during the run of *The American Lady*. I said, 'We are going to sup at the club.' Byron proposed we should wait for Mr. Hingston, the manager. We did. After considerable delay, I said, 'Why does he not come? What is he doing?' 'Oh he's waiting to try and remember if there's anything else he can forget besides our appointment,' said Byron.

"Yes, there are a lot of good stories of Byron," Toole continued; "that about Woodin, who used in his entertainment to go down beneath his rostrum and come up as a countryman, a prima donna, a soldier, a policeman; it was his poly-graphic entertainment, you know: well, at times he was rather a bore, and Byron one night said,

' I wish he would go down and come up somebody else altogether.'

"And that is a little like what he said about Creswick, who was Sheppard's partner at the Surrey. 'Creswick has come back from Australia,' some one said to Byron; 'looks first rate; he has come back quite another man.' 'Hope he hasn't come back Sheppard,' said Byron.

"On another occasion—"

"Time's up," I said, "a page of type is not telescopic nor elastic; and we have come to the last; I regret it; and if the reader is sorry that the end has come, then your Reminiscences have been a great success."

"Thanks to you—"

"Not at all," I said, interrupting him, "thanks to the subject. We have had a pleasant time."

"Very: I hate saying good-bye."

"The best of friends must part," I suggest.

"Not necessarily for good. Can't we make it ' *Au revoir* ? "

" If you prefer it."

"I do. Although we have finished the Reminiscences, they will run at the Libraries, as a good play runs at the theatres—eh ? "

" I hope so,"

" And when the first long run is over, the book

will still be open ; it will be a permanent show, so
to speak.   Is it arrogant to think so ? "

" I hope not."

" I only want a sufficient excuse to avoid saying,
' Good-bye.' "

" Then I will write down the pleasant words,
' *Au revoir !* ' "

"Thanks ; and while I say it, taking the
reader's hand as it were, I would like to recall
the many kind favours I have received at the
hands of pleasant people in the provinces, and
the gratifying social enjoyments they have
afforded me. I do not in this refer to notable
dinners at clubs and hotels, nor to public
receptions, but to the quiet, home-like places
where one is received into the bosom of a
cultivated family, whose sympathies are with the
drama, who love the stage for the good there is in
it, and who appreciate the efforts of actors who
respect and uphold their calling. There are, thank
goodness, such families in every city ; but there is
one I am more particularly thinking of at the present moment,—that of Dr. Pryde, of Edinburgh,
a very learned but simple-minded man, with a
broad and deep knowledge of the literature of the
English stage, and a sincere admiration for the
great artists who have interpreted it.   He and
his charming wife are always more or less asso-

ciated, in my mind, with 'The Vicar of Wakefield.' They are devoted to Irving, and when I last saw them were talking with intense pleasure of *Olivia* and his later work. They always go to the play, mostly with their daughters, and it has generally happened to me, once at least during my Edinburgh engagements, to go home with them to supper; upon which occasions the daughters have sat up, and evidently enjoyed the conversation about the theatre, the higher purposes of the drama, the famous actors the Doctor had seen and known, the remarkable career of Mr. Irving, the old days of Edinburgh playgoing, and so on. And one always pauses to think that if the more cultured people of a city were liberal in their patronage of the drama, nothing would tend more to elevate the stage, and improve the character of the pieces performed, compelling humorists to be wholesome and pure in their fun, and the more serious dramatists and actors to be equally true in their pathos."

INDEX TO VOL. II.

THE END.